THE

ARSENAL

A Dylan Kane Thriller

Also by J. Robert Kennedy

THE ARSENAL

A Dylan Kane Thriller

J. ROBERT KENNEDY

UNDERMILL PRESS

For Tymofiy Mykolayovych Shadura, a Ukrainian prisoner of war murdered in cold blood by Russian invaders. May you rest in peace, and those responsible be brought to justice, in this life and the next.

THE
ARSENAL

A Dylan Kane Thriller

"…in terms of production capacity, China, in many aspects, especially if we talk about ground-forces weapons, might be stronger than Russia and the whole of NATO combined."

Vasily Kashin
Director of the Center for Comprehensive European and International Studies at Moscow's Higher School of Economics

"With respect to sanctions and aid to Russia, we have made clear that providing material support to Russia or assistance with any type of systemic sanctions evasion would be a very serious concern to us."

US Treasury Secretary Janet Yellen

PREFACE

After the Russian invasion of Ukraine, most of the democratic world reacted by imposing severe sanctions on this authoritarian state in an effort to starve it of the funding necessary to conduct the war.

They failed.

Partially.

It is estimated Russia, at the time of this writing, is losing over $175 million per day in fossil fuel exports, however far too many rogue states continue to purchase Russian oil and gas.

Rogue states like China.

NATO member Turkey.

And India.

India, in particular, has been eager to sop up blood oil, with less than 2% of their imports from Russia before the war, now taking in almost 1.6 million barrels per day, each barrel meaning more bullets, more guns, and more bombs, available to kill innocent civilians.

There is no hope for China, however, eventually, one would hope democracies like India and Turkey will see the error of their ways and boycott Russian oil and natural gas as well. These imports, especially India's, where there was no dependence on Russian oil before, are purely greed motivated, and can be stopped by rechecking one's moral compass.

And when that day comes, Russia will truly be brought to its knees.

Then the question becomes, what will the Russian Bear do to protect itself?

Russia

Five Days From Now

CIA Operations Officer Sherrie White cocked an ear toward the heavy gunfire to her left. She recognized the distinctive rattle of AK-74 assault rifles and the crisp report of a Makarov pistol over the clapping of helicopter rotors. The Russians had obviously caught up to her colleague, and she said a silent prayer for him.

There was no way he could survive.

Not against those odds.

Her partner in this, her friend, and her country, were losing the best of what America had to offer the world. He was the quintessential hero and he was dying, sacrificing himself to give her a chance to survive.

And the guilt that knowledge filled her with was overwhelming.

She had to survive, she had to escape, she had to live on so that the gift of life he had given her at the expense of his own wasn't wasted.

Then the gunfire stopped.

The chopper continued to pound at the air and she closed her eyes, saying goodbye to her fallen friend.

CIA Operations Officer Dylan Kane.

Minsk, Belarus

Five Days Earlier

CIA Operations Officer Dylan Kane peered around the corner and spotted his target standing one block away. Ansary Firouz leaned on the hood of his idling car, puffing on what was likely a Cuban cigar. The vermin was an Iranian businessman, an arms broker who not only sold weapons to the highest bidder, but also served as an intermediary between Iran and other foreign powers. He had been on the Agency's watch list for years. Kane had wanted to take him out since the first time he had heard of him, but had been overruled. Because the man was so overconfident, so arrogant, he went to little effort to hide his activities, and Langley felt that could be advantageous at some point.

And perhaps they had been right.

Rumors were flying that Beijing might provide weaponry to Russia, and if they did, it could change the tide of the war and the balance of power. In fact, it could change the entire future of Western Europe. If Russia won in Ukraine, it was only a matter of time before it pushed into additional bordering territories like Moldova, Belarus, Georgia, and other former Soviet republics, and the West would stand by as a rearmed, resupplied Russia would be too expensive to fight.

His question had always been, where was Russia getting the money? As the sanctions continued to bite, their revenues were dropping, though not by as much as the West had hoped, because countries like India and China and others were happy to buy their oil at a discount, despite the innocent blood it represented. Every barrel of oil that a country like India or China bought from the Russians meant the authoritarian regime in Moscow could buy more bullets, more guns, more bombs, to kill the innocent. It disgusted him, and he personally felt it was time for sanctions to be levied against any country that continued to buy Russian resources.

But none of that mattered right now. Right now, he had been assigned to figure out just what the hell Firouz was doing. He had been spotted in Beijing two days ago then in Baghdad yesterday, entering the House of Leadership where the Iranian Ayatollah resided. And today he was in Minsk, the capital of Belarus, Moscow's puppets in their Ukraine offensive. China was well aware that if they did directly sell weapons to Russia, the West might finally grow a backbone and bring in crippling sanctions, so they would likely use an intermediary. Sell the weapons to Iran then Iran sells them to Moscow. But if he could prove the connection before the deal was made, Washington would be able to warn off Beijing.

An SUV pulled up and Firouz pushed off the hood, stubbing out his cigar on the windshield.

Kane activated his comms. "Control, Wild One. We've got activity, over."

His best friend's voice replied in his earpiece. "Copy that, Wild One. We're trying to get an angle on the new arrival. We're repositioning the drone now. Can you get audio?"

"Stand by." Kane reached into his pocket and retrieved a collapsible mic. He fanned out the cone as he activated it, the device automatically pairing with his phone. He aimed it toward the two men as he ducked back behind the corner, staring at the screen, a small red dot indicating where the device was centered.

All he heard was static.

He adjusted slightly as the two men shook hands, and their pleasantries came through loud and clear.

"The new arrival is Dimitri Peskov. He's the Russian president's chief of staff," reported CIA Analyst Supervisor Chris Leroux.

Kane whistled. "In other words, he's the type of person who shouldn't be out alone in this part of town, at this time of night, in this country."

"Agreed."

"Stand by," said Kane as the business side of the conversation began.

"I assume you were successful?"

Firouz nodded. "Extremely. They've agreed to supply everything that you've requested. It'll be hidden through their regular weapons sales to various countries including Iran, and then redirected to you.

The payments will follow the same route. There'll be no direct communication or paper trail between Moscow and Beijing."

"Excellent. And the personal message from the president?"

"Delivered, however, I didn't receive a response before I left."

"So you have nothing for me on that?"

"Only that my contact in Beijing said your president could expect a personal response in the next forty-eight hours, and that was yesterday, so I suspect you'll be hearing something tomorrow."

"Very well."

Firouz stepped closer. "Just what was this personal message?"

"That's none of your concern."

"It is if it involves money. I deserve my commission."

"You're being paid very handsomely. Now's not the time to get greedy."

Firouz chuckled. "Greed is expecting more than what was promised. I merely expect what I agreed to and nothing more. Ten percent for the first six months. If you have some side deal going, all I want is the same."

Peskov regarded the man. "Ten percent of the deal that's currently being negotiated will be enough money to buy your damn country. What could you possibly need more money for?"

"It's not about the money. It's the principle. If I can't trust you, then I can't work with you. And I have a feeling you're going to need my help to make sure the Chinese don't take advantage of you."

Peskov grunted. "Trust me, if they do accept the president's offer, the Chinese won't be a problem."

"So then, there is a deal?"

"You ask too many questions. You know what the Americans say about curiosity."

Firouz stared. "What?"

"It killed the cat." Peskov raised a finger over his right shoulder. A moment later a shot rang out and Firouz collapsed.

Kane pressed against the wall, his eyes immediately surveying the rooftops, searching for the sniper. "Control, any idea where that shot came from? I'm a sitting duck out here."

"Stand by, Wild One. We're reviewing the footage."

Kane folded up the directional microphone, shoving it back in his pocket as he slowly retreated, his back pressed against the building as cover. He reached a doorway and stepped into it, hopefully reducing any angle a sniper might have on him. "Come on, guys. What's the story?"

"Wild One, we've reviewed the footage. He was hit from behind. That sniper should have no angle on you, but that assumes there's only one."

"What's Peskov doing?"

"Looks like he's searching the body and taking Firouz's wallet and other personal items, probably to make it harder to identify him. Okay, he's returning to his SUV. He's heading in your direction." Leroux cursed. "He's turning left. He's going to be crossing right in front of you."

Kane dropped, yanking his jacket up over his head and pulling it over his face as he curled into a ball, huddling in the corner of the door frame, attempting to appear homeless. The SUV passed, the engine fading into the night, and his heart settled.

Slightly.

"You're clear," reported Leroux.

"Am I? What about that sniper?"

"We just spotted another vehicle leaving about half a klick away. We're tracing back where its occupant came from, but he'd be in the right position for the shot that was taken. Stand by."

Kane maintained his homeless pretense, playing out the scenario for himself. If he were Peskov, what size team would he bring? It would be Russian, it would be government. A deal like this couldn't risk outside contractors, no matter how much in bed they were with the regime. Probably Spetsnaz. They typically worked in teams of at least four. The fact that Peskov had come alone without a driver or bodyguard meant he didn't even trust his security team to be exposed to what could be going on.

If it were a CIA op, he would position his team to cover him from all angles, which on this road, bordered on either side by four or five-story buildings, meant two snipers positioned north and south to cover the entire area. Two more would be on the ground so they could rush in should something go wrong that required a more hands-on response. He couldn't see them with less than four, but more risked containment.

"Wild One, Control. We traced the driver to a building just south of you. Computer projection indicates it's likely where the shot came from. He just picked up a second man who we've traced back to a position north of you."

"So just the two?"

"Affirmative."

"Look for two more, probably on the ground, probably very nearby, in a vehicle."

"We're reviewing footage now of another vehicle that was parked one street over. Stand by, something's happening."

Kane tensed. "Care to elaborate?"

"Looks like all three vehicles in question are now heading in the same direction. One of them has already reached Peskov's SUV and taken up position ahead of him. Looks like they're setting up to be his escort."

"Understood. Track him. Let's see where he goes, but my guess is he's heading straight back to Moscow. Any sign of further activity?"

"Negative, Wild One, but I recommend you get out of the area. Somebody probably heard that shot and that body will be spotted sooner rather than later."

Kane rose, straightening his jacket. "Or the Russians will send in a cleanup crew. Either way, you're right. Heading back to my vehicle now. Arrange transport for me to Moscow, and let the Chief know what we just heard. From the way Peskov was talking, it sounds to me whatever side deal they proposed to the Chinese could be even bigger than the weapons deal we've been worried about."

"Any thoughts on what that could be?"

Kane grunted. "Nothing good."

Presidential Executive Office, The Kremlin
Moscow, Russia

Victor Stepanov folded yet another stick of gum in half before popping it in his mouth. He had drunk far too much the night before, and his mouth was ridiculously dry. In between repeated trips to buy bottled water and the inevitable bathroom break that would follow, he was getting little done, though he supposed that wasn't necessarily true.

He was never very busy.

The only reason he had this job was because of who his father was. Alexei Stepanov was what the Western world liked to call an oligarch. His family controlled a huge amount of Russia's mining operations, and they were worth billions, their operations allowed to function smoothly thanks to generous financial and vocal support of the president.

He couldn't count the number of times he had actually met the man growing up, and he, like most Russians, was a huge admirer. When he was nearing graduation, the president had asked him what he wanted to do, and Victor had shrugged, uncertain as to what to say, but because of who had asked the question, he found himself spouting what he expected the man wanted to hear. "I'd like to serve my country in some capacity. I have a knack for languages, perhaps that could be useful."

His mother had seized on his statement. "He's fluent in six languages and can read, write, and speak them all. He might prove invaluable in your office."

The president had politely smiled, merely saying, "Perhaps."

But the day after graduation, he had received an email inviting him for an interview, and a week later he was a junior translator, a position he was certain was created for him. Why would you have a junior person working in the president's office? It meant he rarely had important work to do, beyond translating news articles from various countries someone had flagged might be of interest to the president or his staff.

Today, he hoped the load would be light after last night's outing. One of the senior translators had turned fifty, and despite being relatively new to the office, Victor had been invited out with the group. He had matched the old guard drink for drink, which had proven foolish. If there was one skill Russia's older generation possessed, it was the ability to drink the younger generation under the table with ease.

He had returned home to his luxury apartment provided by his parents, the building mere steps away from the Kremlin where he worked, and had spent much of the night hugging the toilet bowl. Despite that, he had forced himself to arrive at work on time. 8:00 AM. He was rather disappointed to find that his supervisor and guest of honor at last night's outing had called in sick. So had half the damn staff, the other half rolling in late.

The outer door opened and the president's deputy chief of staff, Anton Kozak, entered, gripping a file folder. "Where's Sergie?"

Victor rose at the reference to the birthday boy. "I'm sorry, sir, but he called in sick."

Kozak cursed. "That fat bastard thinks he can hold his liquor, but he can't." He growled, shaking the file folder. "I need a Chinese translator."

"I can translate Chinese."

Kozak regarded him with a frown. "I need someone more senior with a higher security clearance."

Victor shrugged. "I'm sorry, sir. Right now, I'm the only one who can translate Chinese. I think Mr. Shalkov is coming in at noon if it can wait."

"No, it can't." A string of colorful curses erupted before Kozak slapped the file on Victor's desk. "Translate this, paper only, no copies, your eyes only. As soon as you're done, you come directly to my office with it. Understood?"

"Yes, sir." Victor had to pee.

"How long do you think it will take?"

Victor opened the file, flipping through the half-dozen pages. "If it's as important as I think it is, sir, I believe the accuracy of the translation is critical. Two hours?"

"I hope that's an overestimate."

Victor gulped. "I hope so too, sir."

"Fine. Just get the job done as quickly as you can."

"Yes, sir."

Kozak marched out of the office, slamming the door shut, rattling the photo of the president on the wall and causing Victor to flinch. His bladder released slightly and he bore down then raced for the bathroom, leaving the highly confidential file on his desk, a fact he didn't realize until he was hanging out in front of the urinal.

He sprinted back to his desk, finding the file untouched and the office still mostly deserted. He sat and pulled a pad of paper from his desk and a pencil to allow for easier editing. He opened the file folder and flipped past the cover sheet indicating it was a response to a specific message number, no further details provided.

And when he read the first page, his mouth filled with bile and he flipped the folder shut, locking it in his desk, and rushed back to the bathroom.

Sick for an entirely different reason than last night's partying.

CIA Safe House
Moscow, Russia

Kane inventoried the care package left for him at the CIA safe house. Today, he was flying under the radar—no fancy hotels this time. He checked the Makarov pistol, much preferring a Glock, though being caught with a Makarov was a lot less suspicious than a Glock in this part of the world, though if he were caught with anything these days, there would be no talking his way out of it. He would have to kill, or allow himself to be taken.

Not an option he was willing to consider.

Peskov had returned to Moscow immediately, as expected, and Kane was waiting for a face to be delivered by Moscow Station. It was a Hail Mary attempt to find out what this side deal was. Other intelligence assets were gathering the evidence needed to prove to the world what the Chinese and the Russians had planned. Moles within the Iranian VAJA and the Chinese Ministry of Intelligence would take care of that, but it was this personally delivered message that had Washington concerned. Unfortunately, there was simply no way to know what it could be, and they had only one card to play.

The fact Beijing had promised a response today.

There was a knock at his hotel room door, coded. He strolled over and opened it, a young man smiling as he handed Kane a food order from the local equivalent of UberEats. Kane tipped the kid then closed the door, ending the interaction with the Moscow Station employee. He sat the package on the table in the corner and opened it. He removed an order of lasagna, no doubt from the embassy kitchen, and underneath it found another package. He carefully lifted it out then opened it, revealing a Chinese face staring up at him. He gently picked it up and began the process of applying his new face created with state-of-the-art tech perfected over decades. Unless someone physically grabbed at his face, they would never know he was wearing a mask printed less than an hour ago that exactly matched Zhang Wenbin, the Chinese ambassador's attaché, a man that Peskov would recognize, though hopefully didn't know well enough to be familiar with the voice.

He stared at himself in the mirror, never comfortable when the reflection that met his gaze wasn't his own. There was something uncanny about it, almost spooky, as if he were possessing someone else's body.

"Wild One, Control. The call's been placed and the meeting arranged. Peskov is expecting you in one hour at his home to discuss the offer made through Firouz."

"How did he seem?"

"A little confused. He said they already received a reply this morning. Our guy ad-libbed and said there's more to discuss than what was in that reply. You're going to have to bluff your way through it."

Kane grunted as he checked the fit around his ears. "Wasn't that always the plan?" He filled the pockets of his suit with his cover's ID. "When will my driver be here?"

"He's ten minutes out with VIN and tags that match a car registered with the Chinese embassy in case Peskov's people do their jobs a little more thoroughly than we're expecting. The briefing on his regular security suggests it's fairly light. I get the distinct impression he doesn't expect trouble at home."

Somebody said something in the background at the operations center. "Stand by, Wild One."

Kane continued his prep then practiced his Russian with a Chinese accent, mimicking Zhang's voice as best he could. Matching a voice unfamiliar to another person needn't be an exact science. It was their demeanor and tone that were more important. If Peskov had heard Zhang speak in the past, he would expect someone who spoke in a similar manner. If Kane walked in there boisterous and confident, when Zhang was traditionally demure, as he was, Peskov might grow suspicious.

Leroux returned. "Wild One, Control. We might have a situation here."

"Report."

"We got lucky. Someone at Peskov's residence used their landline to call the Chinese embassy to confirm the meeting. We had someone tap the line earlier today, so we were able to reroute and confirm the meeting. It suggests they're suspicious."

"Yeah, it does, doesn't it? I guess I'll have to be super-duper careful rather than just super careful like I usually am."

Leroux chuckled. "Yeah, you're famous for being careful."

Kane headed for the bathroom, not sure when he would get his next chance. "Control, signing off, unless you want to hear me hang ten and drain the main vein."

"Appreciate the warning. Good luck."

Kane unzipped his fly. "What are you talking about? I do this all the time."

Operations Center 3, CIA Headquarters
Langley, Virginia

Leroux leaned back at his station as Kane's comms fell silent. "I don't have a good feeling about this."

His second in command, Sonya Tong, turned in her chair to face him. "Neither do I. There's no way this is going to work. There has to be another way."

Leroux shrugged. "I'm open to suggestions, but I can't see any other way. This is something so classified, they hand-delivered it by paper through a third-party envoy. Any further communications are going to be either direct or through their hotline. That's impossible for us to tap. We need somebody sitting in the room, or we need someone in the know to talk. The only way we can get someone to talk is either by tricking them or by beating it out of them, and at the moment, the only person we're aware of who knows what's going on is Peskov. And that'd be like the Russians beating the shit out of the White House

Chief of Staff to get answers. There's just no way we can do it. Tricking him is the only option."

Danny Packman cleared his throat. "Sir, he's getting in the car now."

Leroux glanced at the screen to see the satellite footage showing the car pulling away from the safe house. It would pass through a camera dead zone near the Chinese embassy, where the plates would flip to those matching the embassy-registered car, just in case the Russians were extra cautious.

He was nervous for his friend. If Kane were caught, there was no telling what might happen. If there was some secret deal under negotiation between the Russians and the Chinese, they might decide eliminating him was their only option, rather than imprisoning him for a future exchange of a Russian asset.

"We could try to plant a bug," suggested the tech wunderkind of the team, Randy Child.

Leroux dismissed the idea. "His home and offices are swept probably half a dozen times daily."

"I'm not talking about a traditional bug. I'm talking micro-drones. Land them on the windows, listen to the vibrations, pick up the conversations. When they go to scan the room, detach, fly away, come back."

Leroux again dismissed the idea. "Won't work. As soon as the Russians caught wind we had those, they began installing infrared sweepers on all their key windows. As soon as the drones are detected breaking the beam, the jig's up."

"But at his house? Surely they haven't installed those detectors there yet."

"We don't know if they have, but we can't take the risk. If Kane's in there and they detect the drone, he's screwed. And if he doesn't go in, the chances of Peskov talking about the agreement at home are next to nil. At the moment, the only hope we have is Kane."

Peskov Residence

Moscow, Russia

Dimitri Peskov sat at his desk and ran his hand across the surface, his fingertips detecting the bumps and gouges from over a century of use by the eldest sons of his family. His father had passed three years ago and it had been a bittersweet day when the family heirloom arrived. Just having it here brought back so many memories as a child watching his father working behind it. Now it was his, and he wondered if the affairs of state he now dealt with while seated at it were ever matched by those of his ancestors.

He somehow doubted it.

The proposal to the Chinese would have been unthinkable just a year ago, and when it had been proposed during a brainstorming session, it had been immediately rejected by everyone in the room. But when the meeting had adjourned and he had followed the president to his office, the moment the doors closed he had been ordered to look into it.

It was a brilliant plan. Russia's wealth came from its natural resources—oil, natural gas, its massive capacity at producing wheat and other grains. But it did have an immensely valuable unmatched resource that was incredibly expensive to maintain, and with the sanctions increasingly crippling their economy having no end in sight, it was an asset they could no longer afford. There were others out there, allies, who could afford to maintain this asset. The question was would they be willing to take it off their hands?

The response received this morning certainly suggested the Chinese were willing, and in fact eager.

He was curious why they were sending their attaché in person, though he supposed it made sense. If the Americans caught wind of this, there was no telling what the response would be. This would fundamentally and permanently shift the balance of power in the region. Should this go through successfully, the Chinese would never fear America again, and America could never possibly challenge her militarily.

Things would never be the same.

And while that was good for China, it was also good for Mother Russia. His country would save untold billions, but also receive massive payments for the next thirty years, and an ally that would guarantee his country's protection. No longer would America and its Western allies dictate what was permissible outside their borders. Their new power bloc would be unrivaled in history, and would change the way of the world, ending Western nonsense.

He wept that it had come to this, but rejoiced that his country had a leader strong enough and wise enough to realize what was necessary to secure their country's legacy, during which time they would rebuild and reemerge even stronger than before, while the West collapsed in upon itself as its binary society tore itself apart, not recognizing who its true enemies were.

The doorbell rang and he glanced at the clock on the wall, another family heirloom liberated by his great-grandfather during the fall of Berlin in World War II, an intricate affair handcrafted in the Black Forest of Germany. His Chinese guest was right on time. He headed for the front entrance of his home, his stomach churning. This meeting could prove critical, and he had to be careful what was said.

A meeting at his home was highly unusual, which was why he had his assistant confirm it. Things were at a critical juncture. Nothing had been signed, but things were ready to roll, facilities across the country already prepping. He couldn't screw this up.

He could hear his aide greeting their visitor and he forced a smile as he rounded the corner. He extended a hand and Zhang shook it before stepping back and bowing. Peskov returned the gesture, recognizing the man. "It's good to see you again."

Kane silently cursed at the revelation they had met. "Likewise," he replied. This could be about to prove difficult, and he thanked God he had Leroux in his ear.

"Peskov attended a Chinese embassy function two weeks ago, celebrating the Chinese New Year. You would've been there."

"Chinese New Year, wasn't it?"

Peskov led him deeper into the house. "A delightful event. I'm certain I speak for all Russians who were fortunate enough to attend that it was the highlight of the year."

Kane bowed slightly as they entered Peskov's office. "I am honored, and will pass your compliments on to the ambassador."

Peskov indicated two comfortable leather chairs. "Can I get you anything?"

"No, I'm fine, thank you."

Peskov sat across from him. "And how is your wife?"

Leroux immediately spoke. "She's in Beijing visiting her ailing mother. She wasn't at the party. He could be testing you."

Kane sighed, flicking a wrist. "She remains at her mother's side. I fear I'm torn between wanting my wife back with me, and my mother-in-law to recover and live for many more good years."

Peskov grunted. "The obligations of family only double when one gets married."

Kane's head bobbed. "This is true." So far, he didn't get a sense that he had raised any suspicions. Unless Peskov was playing him, it was clear the man wasn't familiar with the real Zhang's voice. Kane leaned forward. "I'm certain you're a busy man, and I don't want to waste too much of your personal time."

"You'll find Russia always has time for its Chinese friends."

"And you'll find that China is always appreciative of that time. And this proposed new agreement between our two great nations will only further solidify the bonds already established between our two countries."

"Indeed. I can convey that the president was quite pleased with your reply this morning agreeing in principle to our terms."

Kane's mind raced. He had no clue what the hell was going on and had to speak in vagaries that didn't make him sound like a moron. "And I can assure you my president was equally pleased to read the proposal passed by our mutual, shall we say, friend, Mr. Firouz."

Peskov shifted in his chair. Kane had dropped the name to add legitimacy to his cover, for few would know he was involved. The Chinese definitely shouldn't know that Peskov had ordered the man's execution the night before. The Belarusian authorities had found the body, and reports already indicated they were chalking it up to a mugging gone bad. The fact no one was questioning why it was a high-powered sniper rifle that had put a hole in the man suggested the Russians had told the Belarusians what should be said. "It's a shame what happened to him."

"Crime is a plague the world over."

Peskov agreed. "Indeed. Perhaps when our two countries hold the balance of power, we can get even firmer in our approach to criminal activity."

"Perhaps. I suppose, however, it's fortunate that there's one less person out there who knows what's going on."

Peskov smiled slightly, perhaps enjoying the inside joke he thought he was the only one in on. "I guess that's one way of looking at it. This is, of course, extremely sensitive. If the Americans were to find out, they would certainly try to stop it."

"Agreed. Time is of the essence here," was the only thing Kane could think to say. Time was always of the essence, so it was a relatively safe observation.

"Yes, it is, which is why we've already begun preparing for the transfer. We have hundreds of mobile assets already being readied. The moment the agreement is signed and the initial payment is made, we're prepared to transfer fifty units by rail with the first arriving within forty-eight hours."

Kane was dying to ask just what these units were, yet he couldn't. "That sounds acceptable. The faster we get the transfer done, the less chance there is of American interference."

"Exactly. And once that initial transfer is complete, the Americans won't dare interfere. The retaliation could be devastating. Did you have any further questions? Anything you want to take to my president?"

Kane sensed Peskov wanted to end the meeting. "No. And do you have any for mine?"

"No."

Kane rose. "Then I suggest we leave any further negotiations to our leaders." He extended his hand. "I look forward to a mutually beneficial future."

Peskov grasped Kane's hand in both of his, squeezing firmly. "A future no longer dominated by America, but by China and Russia."

The door burst open and Peskov's aide rushed in, his eyes wide. He stabbed a finger at Kane. "That's not the attaché!"

Kane didn't bother denying it. His hand darted out and he crushed Peskov's windpipe, not enough to kill him, just enough to take him out of the equation for the next few minutes.

"Guards!" shouted the aide as Kane closed the three steps between them and reached out, grabbing the man by the neck and twisting him around before putting him in a sleeper hold. Footfalls in the hallway had him pressing his back against the wall by the door then releasing the aide's unconscious form. The first of what Langley had assured him were no more than four guards entered the room, his gun leading the way. Kane reached out and broke the man's grip, grabbing the weapon as it fell. His foot darted out, catching the man on his side, sending him crashing into the door. Kane put two rounds in his chest then dropped down and leaned into the doorway, firing two more into a second guard.

"Control, Wild One. We've got a situation here," he said as he leaped to his feet and rushed down the hallway, grabbing another weapon off the second guard. Shouts from the household erupted as more panic and concern set in. He headed for the front door as Leroux responded.

"The security system's been activated by the looks of it. We've got two guards with weapons on the car. Armed response is likely no more than five minutes away. What's your status?"

Kane continued for the front door. He didn't bother grabbing his jacket taken from him when he had arrived. Peskov's wife stepped into the hallway and she gasped, her eyes bulging at Kane. "Stay back," he warned her, and her hands shot up as she retreated. He continued to the door, an alarm sounding, and he shoved it open, stepping out into the frigid cold. One of the exterior guards had his back to him, advancing on the car. Kane put two in his back then two in his buddy on the other side before jumping in the disguised Chinese embassy vehicle. "Let's get the hell out of here!"

"You don't have to tell me twice," replied his driver, putting the car in gear and hammering on the gas.

"Control, report."

Leroux replied. "No signs of pursuit, but local authorities are responding. Take your next right."

Kane pointed for the benefit of the driver, who couldn't hear Leroux's end of the conversation. "Go right."

The driver executed the turn then reached forward, pressing a combination of buttons on the dash. The Chinese flags flying at the corners of the hood retracted.

"Okay, Control. You've got to get us to a switch point ASAP. This whole area's going to be crawling before you know it."

"Feeding coordinates to your GPS now."

The GPS on the dash beeped, a new destination appearing. His driver took a quick glance at the screen. "We'll be there in six minutes, but I can do it in four."

Kane dismissed the idea. "No. Obey the speed limit. We don't want to do anything to attract attention." As if to punctuate his point, two police cars whipped past, their sirens wailing, their lights flashing.

His driver eased off the gas, tucking in behind another car. "Driving Miss Daisy mode engaged."

Kane chuckled as he checked for any pursuers.

"Wild One, Control. An APB has just gone out for a vehicle matching your description. They've got your plates, over."

"Copy that, Control." He glanced at the driver. "Plates?"

"Switched."

"Control, confirming our plates have been switched." He glanced at the GPS. "ETA three minutes to switch point."

More squad cars zipped past, two screeching to a halt just as they cleared an intersection. His driver glanced in his rearview mirror. "They're setting up a roadblock. Looks like we just got outside their perimeter." He pointed ahead. "There it is."

"Killing the cameras now," said Leroux in his ear as they pulled into a public parking garage. "Second level, black Toyota SUV. Last three digits of the plate are seven-one-two."

Kane relayed the info and they wound their way to the second level. He pointed. "There it is."

They parked and Kane climbed out, heading over to the SUV and retrieving the keys from the rear driver's side wheel well as his driver pressed a combination on the key fob to their old car, activating a chemical mist that would dissolve anything organic, leaving no DNA or other traceable evidence behind. Kane fired up the engine and they pulled out of the parking garage and onto the road, heading away from the ever-increasing security.

"Looks like we got away," said his driver, now passenger.

Kane checked the rearview mirror. "For now."

"Was it worth it?"

Kane shrugged. He still had no idea what this was about, though he had his suspicions, and they worried him. He glanced over at his companion. "I honestly don't know how to answer that."

Peskov Residence

Moscow, Russia

Peskov held his sobbing wife, gently stroking her hair in an effort to calm her as security personnel swarmed his home. Four men were dead, men he didn't know well, but still knew by name. He had never experienced anything like this before. There were a lot of generals and colonels he had met over the years due to his position that were now dead, killed on the battlefield, but that was different. That was a death he read about in a report. Never had he seen them getting killed. And death on the battlefield was one thing. Death inside his own home on such a scale was an entirely different matter.

His aide, Vladislav Medinsky, entered the room.

"Vlad, are you all right?" Peskov winced, his throat still sore from where the infiltrator had punched him. He massaged it as Medinsky shrugged.

"The doctor says I'll live."

Peskov's wife reached out and squeezed Medinsky's arm. "Thank God for that." She wiped her eyes dry with a knuckle. "I'm going to go check on the children. What should I tell them?"

Peskov chewed his cheek for a moment. "They'll hear about it at school, for sure. Just tell them that somebody pretending to be someone else came into our home, the deception was discovered and the security team did its job protecting us. In the process, we lost four good men who died heroes. The imposter got away, but will be found. Tell them they're safe now and that security will be increased to make sure it never happens again."

She sighed. "Why would the Chinese do this?"

"We don't know it was the Chinese. They all look the same. He could have been Chinese, North Korean, Japanese. Our country has a lot of enemies, and sometimes even those who claim to be our friends aren't always so. We'll figure it out, don't worry. Now, go check on the children, tell them I'll be up to see them as soon as I can."

She pushed up on her toes and gave him a peck on his cheek then left the room.

Medinsky stepped closer, lowering his voice. "Who do you think it was?"

"I don't know." Peskov paused, replaying the events. There had been little time to review what had happened, and he twigged on a memory. "Wait. When you came in, you said he wasn't who he said he was. How did you know?"

Medinsky wagged his phone. "Something wasn't sitting right with the meeting. It just seemed so out of the ordinary, so I ran his name just to confirm." He brought up a picture showing Zhang at an embassy function. "Looks like him, doesn't it?"

"Absolutely, there's no doubt it's the same man."

"Well, unless he has a twin, our man is wearing Oscar-winning makeup, because the real Zhang left for Beijing yesterday to join his wife."

"And he's still there?"

"I'm having it looked into, but yes, I believe so."

Peskov took the phone and stared at the picture. It was definitely the same man. He regarded Medinsky. "*Does* he have a twin?"

"According to our files, he's an only child, like most from China."

Peskov pursed his lips and handed the phone back. He had heard of the Americans' capability of printing faces, but had never seen it first-hand. This had to be a case of that, and it was technology so well-guarded he wasn't certain it was shared with their allies. And if it were, it would be only those they truly trusted, like the Brits.

"What do you think this is all about? What was he trying to find out?"

Peskov dismissed the question. Medinsky wasn't privy to what was going on, beyond that there *was* something going on. He was aware of the weapons deal, but not of the secret side deal entrusted to Firouz. "Classified."

"Understood. Do you have any instructions?"

Peskov folded his arms and stared out the window at the flashing lights of the emergency vehicles. "Confirm that Zhang is in Beijing and that he doesn't have a twin. Then focus on tracking that car, where it went, where it came from. Also, see if you can trace the call that came here to make the appointment. I can think of only a handful of people who are aware of what is going on, and this man knew. We have a leak somewhere and we need to plug it fast."

"Yes, sir. I'll coordinate with Director Nikitin. He's on his way personally."

"Very well." Peskov dismissed his aide with a flick of the wrist then headed up the stairs to check on his children, pausing on the landing as he replayed the conversation he had had with the imposter. He was assuming that the man knew the contents of the letter, but had he? The start of the conversation was diplomatic babble, then he had given the man details. Fifty units starting within forty-eight hours. The imposter had said little. Could this have been a fishing expedition? Could the Americans or some other party be aware of the letter but not its contents, so they sent someone in?

Peskov's blood ran cold at the idea. What had he actually said? What had he revealed? Fifty units starting within forty-eight hours. He remembered that distinctly, but had he referred to what those units were? He shut his eyes as he reached up and squeezed his forehead. He should have known something was going on, but it had never occurred to him anyone could know what was truly happening. He wasn't exaggerating when he said perhaps half a dozen people in Russia, and likely the same in China, knew about the side agreement.

If word had somehow gotten out, it could jeopardize everything. The question was, where was the leak? There were only three possible sources he could think of—the Chinese, someone at his end, or Firouz himself. Firouz was the most obvious choice, but if he had opened the letter, he wouldn't have been asking the questions that got him killed.

His eyes shot wide at a sudden realization. Firouz was known to the intelligence community, which meant somebody might have been following him to see why he was in Belarus. Someone could have been listening to their conversation and witnessed the execution. It would explain how they would know to contact him and not someone else, and know of the existence of the letter.

It explained everything. And if it were true, it meant they had no leak. Unfortunately, there was no way to prove it either way. They would still have to go on a mole hunt. Right now, everyone was a possible source, and if the Americans did suspect something, they had little time to complete their deal with the Chinese, for if it were exposed, there was no way Beijing would proceed.

And Russia's future would remain uncertain.

CIA Safe House
Moscow, Russia

Kane flopped on his bed, exhausted. They had bounced around the city, switching cars four times, losing their faces on the second. Moscow Station had vehicles all over the city for just these situations. On the second switch, he had parted ways with his driver, whom Langley had just reported had passed through the embassy gates driving a car with plates that matched the one he had left in earlier in the evening.

He grabbed the remote control and turned on the TV, switching to the local news, not that he expected any truth out of it, since everything was government-controlled. He watched for about a minute but there was no mention of what had happened earlier. The Russians were probably trying to figure out what spin to put on it, if any. They might just bury the story, as it was a humiliating security breach.

He activated his comms. "Control, Wild One. Any update?"

Leroux responded. "Negative, Wild One. Do you have time for a debrief?"

Kane sighed. "I suppose."

"Any theories as to what this is all about?"

Kane sat on the edge of the bed, staring at himself in the mirror. "He kept referring to units, and the ability to move fifty of them starting within forty-eight hours. The question is what the hell are these units?"

"We've been mulling that over at this end as well. If they're talking about transferring fifty units of something, starting within forty-eight hours from locations across the country, and transferring them to China, it can't be personnel. It has to be a physical asset."

"Agreed, but what could Russia be transferring to China? Russia is desperate for weapons. What do the Russians have that they don't need, and that the Chinese want? Or, I suppose, more accurately, don't have enough of?"

"Well, Randy has a theory. He thinks they're talking about hypersonic missiles, since the quantities are so low yet they're referred to as mobile, and the implication is that they're valuable."

Kane's eyebrows shot up at the idea. It had occurred to him as well, but hearing someone else say it made it sound all the more ominous. "Now, that's a definite possibility. It's tech the Chinese don't have and would desperately want."

"They did refer to fifty units starting within forty-eight hours located across the country. That would be about the number we think they actually have, but our numbers could be wrong. They might have more."

Kane stood, pacing in front of the muted television. "Okay, let's think about this. The Russians are desperate for money and weapons. Their hypersonic missiles are too damn expensive to use in big numbers, and they can't afford to build them. The Chinese are drowning in money, so offer to foot the bill. Russia manufactures the missiles on Beijing's dime, handing over what they manufacture as part of the partnership, holding back some so they can use them on the battlefield. Both sides win. Ukraine loses."

"That makes sense," agreed Leroux. "It would be a side deal they couldn't risk doing through an intermediary. Bullets and Kalashnikovs are one thing. You can pass those through the Iranians or the North Koreans or whoever. But hypersonic missiles are just too tempting. You know if the North Koreans or the Iranians got access to them, a few would fall off the back of the truck, and neither China nor Russia would want countries like that gaining access to that kind of technology."

"So, what do we do about it?"

"I'm not sure. And we can't even be sure that we are talking about hypersonic missiles. I'm going to brief the Chief, and I have no doubt he'll talk to Washington. I suggest you get some sleep, and we'll have more to tell you in the morning. Leave your earpiece in, though. You might get a wake-up call."

"Copy that. Good night."

Leroux yawned. "Do you have any idea what time it is here? Sweet dreams to both of us."

Victor Stepanov Residence

Moscow, Russia

Victor sat on a stool at his breakfast bar, powering down a large serving of oatmeal as he scrolled through his tablet, connected to the Internet through a VPN that disguised who and where he was. It allowed him to access international news feeds, though he usually used it to access a friend's Netflix account in America. This morning, however, he was seeking the truth. He had a decision to make. The document he had been tasked to translate yesterday had been shocking, and he simply couldn't believe his country had become so desperate to enter into such an agreement. If things were going as well in Ukraine as the president claimed, then there should be no need for such a deal.

But what he was finding was heartbreaking. America was his country's traditional enemy, so he was ignoring any American news sources. Instead, he was focusing on British, German, and French. All the reporting was consistent between news organizations and countries.

If the rest of the world was to be believed, it was clear his country was the aggressor, had attacked first, was committing unspeakable atrocities, that there was no fascist government in Ukraine, and that it was all a lie.

Yet he couldn't believe it. He respected the president, admired him, thought of him as a hero. Men like that didn't lie to people, not to this extent.

He pulled up another video making the rounds and flinched as a Ukrainian prisoner smoking a cigarette was shot. Executed. He dropped the tablet, his oatmeal forgotten. What he had just witnessed was a war crime. Murder. There was no denying it. And there could be no possible context in which it was legitimate. Could it be staged? Could it be faked? Could the Ukrainians have executed their own man? All these things were possible, but when taken together with everything he had just read, and what he had read all yesterday evening, he was certain the truth as he had been told was a lie.

He eyed the tiny memory card sitting on the counter in front of him. He had done something insane yesterday, something that could get him executed for treason, but at the time, he had felt he had no choice. He had used his phone to photograph the pages of the document. At the time, he wasn't sure why he was doing it. He simply felt compelled to. He had considered showing it to his father, for surely he would agree that what was proposed went too far, but after sober reflection, he had decided against it. His father was too ardent a supporter of the president.

Last night, he had run through a list of everyone he knew, and he could think of no one he could pass the information on to. He had friends who would be equally outraged, but showing it to them would be pointless, as there was nothing they could do to help. Unfortunately, there was no one individual he could think of that might be able to do something about this.

But there was a country.

America.

The very thought sickened him. To help his country's enemy against his own, a country he still loved, despite what he had discovered, was unthinkable, but there was no one else who could do something to stop what he had read.

The question was, how could he possibly pass the information on? He couldn't exactly walk into the American embassy—it was under constant watch. He would be spotted immediately, his face run against the database, and he would be arrested the moment he walked out. But if he did somehow pass the information on clandestinely, how long would it be before his own people figured out he was behind the leak should the Americans take action?

He would have to leave his country in order to save it.

His eyes pooled with tears at the thought, but he could see no other choice.

The president had to be stopped.

Director Morrison's Office, CIA Headquarters
Langley, Virginia

Leroux struggled to stifle a yawn, failing miserably. Morrison appeared just as tired as he felt.

"When's the last time you got any sleep?"

Leroux shrugged. "I had four hours in the rack, but I don't know if I slept for more than an hour. Every time I lie down and close my eyes, my mind just starts to go."

Morrison leaned back and folded his arms. "I feel the same. I might have got an hour or two as well. Randy will be happy to know that the Pentagon concurs with his theory that the units in question are hypersonic missiles. Washington isn't too happy with us, however."

Leroux's eyes narrowed. "Oh?"

"Well, we assured them they didn't have more than maybe fifty or sixty of those missiles. If they're going to be able to deliver fifty of them starting in two days, keep a supply for their war effort, and deliver hundreds more in the not-too-distant future, then they've got a stash somewhere we don't know about."

"I just can't believe they're doing this. Selling off their showcase weapon, the one thing they have that we don't, the one weapon we can't defend against."

"Washington thinks there's more going on here. The reason the Russians don't have many of these missiles in their armory is because they're too damn expensive to make, especially with the chip restrictions. Washington thinks Beijing will be overpaying to have the Russians manufacture more of them, plus supplying the missing components, and the Russians will use the profits to restock their own supply. It's likely a long-term agreement. Basically, the Chinese will be funding the Russian weapons program, and both sides will reap the rewards. If the Russians had a steady supply of hypersonic missiles at their disposal, it could change the course of the war. The Ukrainians wouldn't be able to defend against them, and the Russians could take out any target they wanted at will. They could keep the Ukrainian power grid and water supply permanently offline across the entire country, and there'd be nothing we could do to stop them. Life would become untenable for tens of millions of Ukrainian civilians, and they'd be demanding their leadership sue for peace."

Leroux's face creased with a frown. "A terrifying thought."

"Indeed."

"What are Washington's orders?"

"They want the deal stopped, but they need proof. Right now, we've got nothing. Everything is an interpretation of a very brief conversation between Peskov and a known Iranian arms dealer, and Kane and the man's executioner. We have no documentation, nothing that we can show to the UN or threaten the Chinese with. We need some sort of proof."

"Like photos of ballistic missiles being set up in Cuban jungles?"

"Exactly. He referred to sites all across the country with stockpiles of these missiles. We need to find those sites and get someone in there to take photos."

"And by someone, you mean Kane."

"Who else?"

Presidential Executive Office, The Kremlin

Moscow, Russia

Victor sat at his desk with a death grip on his mouse, staring blankly at a New York Times article he was translating. It involved the Western push to ban TikTok and whether the concern was justified. He personally didn't have it on his own phone, though a lot of his friends did. His father had explained how anyone who would have that app on their device was a fool. Claims that none of the servers were within China, therefore your data was secure, were nonsense. His father had explained about the National Intelligence Law in China, where the executives of the company behind TikTok were located.

It meant the entire company was subject to the law, and that law essentially stated that if the government of China requested data be handed over, it had to be handed over. It didn't matter if the servers were elsewhere. Chinese law trumped international law, and certainly trumped American privacy laws. They had already proven there were back doors into the data from within China. All it would take would be for a Communist Party official to whisper in a ByteDance executive's ear, and if that executive wanted to see the light of day again, he would comply with the order, meaning the communist government of a totalitarian state would have full access to everything over a billion regular users posted. It had already been shown that TikTok used far more data than a typical social media app for the same functions. Why that was, he didn't know, but he had heard enough from those who did to make certain he avoided the app like the plague.

Before he had headed for work, news had broken about an attack last night on the home of the president's chief of staff, Dimitri Peskov. Two of his staff had been murdered, two others wounded, but the gunman, believed to be a Ukrainian terrorist, had been killed, getting nowhere near Peskov or his family.

And that was why he was shocked to see the prominent bruise on Peskov's neck when the door to the translation office opened and he stepped inside. Everyone rose out of respect, though Victor was certain it had more to do with fear.

Sergie, this week's birthday boy, rose from his desk. "How can I help you, sir?"

"You handle our Chinese translations, correct?"

"Yes, sir."

"Then I need you to come with me."

"Is there a particular document you're concerned with?"

"One from yesterday."

Victor's stomach flipped and his mouth filled with bile, his heart hammering, his ears pounding.

"But I wasn't in yesterday. Are you sure the document was translated by me?"

Peskov stared at the rotund man. "Wait a minute. Our lead Chinese translator wasn't at work yesterday?"

Sergie shifted uncomfortably. "I was feeling poorly, sir. The birthday celebrations got rather out of control."

"Then who would've translated it?"

The truth would come out. If he sat here saying nothing while a conversation within earshot that concerned him took place, they would surely know something was wrong. He gulped down then rose. "Excuse me, sirs, I'm not sure which document you're referring to, however, Mr. Kozak had me translate something for him yesterday morning."

Peskov eyed him. "Who are you?"

"Victor Stepanov."

A flash of recognition momentarily crossed Peskov's face. "Wait a minute, Alexei's son?"

"Yes, sir."

Peskov dismissed the idea. "There's no way you'd have security clearance high enough for this."

"I was the only one available, sir. Everyone was, well, off sick. I was made aware of how important it was to keep it secret and not to discuss it with anyone. I get a sense from what I'm hearing, that it's the same document you're concerned with."

Peskov frowned then beckoned him. "Come with me."

Victor forced himself to follow one of the most important men in Russia, a man who could have him killed with a mere nod, a man who had the complete trust of their president. Someone must have figured out he had photographed the pages, but that didn't make sense. They would have simply come for him directly. Instead, they had come for whoever had translated the document. That could mean there was a leak and they were attempting to figure out who had been exposed to the information, or it could simply be routine. Considering the subject matter, they might want to know who was aware of the agreement, just as a matter of course. The best thing he could do now, the only thing, was to be completely honest, leaving out, of course, the fact he had photographed the pages. Everything else had been by the book.

They boarded the elevator in silence and Victor's nerves continued to get the better of him, compelling him to say something to sound innocent. "Sir, I heard on the news this morning what happened last night. I hope your family wasn't too upset."

Peskov regarded him for a moment. "Fortunately, the terrorist never made it to the second floor where we all were. Everyone will probably be on edge for a couple of weeks, then it will be forgotten."

"Yes, sir, I'm sure that's true. At least the terrorist no longer poses a threat."

Peskov's eyebrows shot up as if puzzled by the statement. "Oh, yes, you're right, at least there's that."

The doors opened and Victor followed Peskov toward a conference room at the far end of the hall, puzzled. The man's reaction suggested the official story being reported wasn't true, that the terrorist wasn't dead. And if that part of the story was a lie, how much of the rest was? The terrorist never made it to the second floor where the entire family was. If that were true, why did Peskov look like he had been punched in the throat?

Something more was going on here, and he suspected it was why they were looking for the translator of yesterday's reply from the Chinese. Was whoever had attacked Peskov's residence last night after information about the document? It made sense. If the information had somehow leaked, then someone might have indeed attempted to find out more from one of the few men in the country who would know the details. It meant there was someone out there on the right side of this who was obviously trying to stop it.

It had to be the Americans. The very notion that it was a Ukrainian terrorist was nonsense. Every crime these days was blamed on Ukrainians. And since the war began, a record number of Russian executives had been killed in mysterious falls. It was a running joke among his friends, though only behind closed doors. No one dared speak of it in public. He distinctly remembered the day his father had said at the dinner table, in all seriousness, "If I ever die from a fall, you'll know I was murdered."

That had settled it for him. And with the fact people so powerful could be murdered by those in charge without a second thought, he had to wonder if they would even think twice about killing the son of one of their allies.

The doors opened and Victor's heart nearly stopped when he saw the director of the FSB, Ilya Nikitin, sitting at the far end of a table surrounded by file folders and a laptop.

He regarded Victor, clearly puzzled. "Who's this?"

"This is the person who translated the document," explained Peskov.

"A child?"

Victor bristled but chose his battles.

Peskov explained. "Apparently, everyone else was out sick, so he was tasked."

"Well, if that's not a breach of security, I don't know what is."

"Agreed." Peskov turned to Victor. "Do you know who this man is?"

"Yes, sir, Director Nikitin, head of the FSB."

"Very good. He's going to ask you a series of questions. Those questions surround the document you were given to translate yesterday, not the contents of it. You will not mention what was in that document to the director, nor will he ask you what the contents are. Understood?"

Victor trembled. "Yes, sir."

"Very well. When you're done, come see me in my office."

"Yes, sir."

Peskov left, closing the door behind him. Nikitin pointed to a nearby chair. "Sit. This shouldn't take long."

"Thank you, sir." Victor took the seat then gripped the armrests. He let go then folded his arms, again second-guessing himself, struggling to figure out what would make him appear innocent. Open pose? He sucked in a breath and leaned back, crossing a leg and gently resting his arms on the armrests, this time foregoing the death grip.

"You appear nervous."

Victor gulped then leaned forward, abandoning his carefully composed demeanor. "To be perfectly honest, sir, if your twenty-two-year-old self were sitting in a room alone with the head of the FSB, wouldn't you be nervous?"

Nikitin laughed. "I'd be shitting my pants."

"Well, sir, fortunately for both of us, I've managed to avoid that so far."

Nikitin roared with laughter. "I like you, kid. And if I'm not mistaken, I see a little bit of Alexei Stepanov behind those eyes. Am I correct?"

"Yes, sir. He's my father."

"I thought the name was familiar, and it's probably the only way a twenty-two-year-old would get a job in this office. Exciting?"

Victor nodded, growing a little more comfortable, the man not at all what he had expected. "Yes, sir, very."

"It's exciting being in the know, isn't it? Seeing things, hearing things that none of your friends are privy to."

"It is, sir. Frustrating at times, of course, since I can't share any of it. But it is fun sometimes to hear a friend give his opinion on something and know they're completely wrong."

"Do you ever correct them?"

"Never, sir. Ever since I took the job, I've learned not to talk politics with my friends. That being said, until yesterday, I've never been exposed to anything that I ever thought was actually a secret."

"Ah, yes, the document that must not be spoken of. Do you know why I'm here?"

Victor continued with his honesty-was-best approach. "If I had to hazard a guess, it has something to do with what happened at Mr. Peskov's residence last night."

Nikitin smiled. "Very astute. And what do you think happened?"

Victor shifted uncomfortably.

"It's all right, tell me what you're thinking."

"I think the news story was less than accurate."

Nikitin chuckled. "You mean the fact that a terrorist was killed before he could even get to the floor where the family was, yet the patriarch of the family has a bruised neck?"

"Something like that, sir."

"Well, obviously we can't have the public worrying that its senior officials can be attacked, and the truth, of course, is a state secret that you won't be discussing with anyone."

"Of course not."

"So, this document. There's a theory that the so-called terrorist might have been after it or been aware of its existence. Tell me everything that's happened since you were asked to translate it."

"Mr. Kozak entered the room looking for a translator. I was the only one there who handled Chinese, so I was tasked with it. He told me how classified it was and that I was to translate it on paper only, then immediately report to him. No copies were to be made. No one was to be shown the document and no one told of the document."

"So, you made your translation. Was there anyone else in the room?"

"Yes, sir. Some people started to arrive later, but I didn't speak to any of them. I simply did my translation, then went to Mr. Kozak's office."

"So, no one saw the document?"

"No, sir."

"Did you ever leave the document unattended?"

"No, sir." He hesitated.

Stick to the truth. There could be video footage.

"Actually, that's not true, sir. I desperately needed to pee. As soon as Mr. Kozak left the room, I headed to the bathroom, not thinking, and I left the folder unattended on my desk. I was only gone maybe three minutes, and when I returned it was exactly where I had left it. And again, at that time, there was nobody in the room."

"Nobody?"

"Well, I guess I should say there was nobody who could read Chinese. I really don't think anyone would've dared open the file because it was marked Classified. If anything, they would've reported me for breaking the rules."

"I agree. Then what happened?"

"I translated it."

"How long did that take?"

"About an hour-and-a-half."

"And then?"

"I took the translation and the original file to Mr. Kozak's office and handed it to him. He read the translation, reminded me that it was highly classified and I wasn't to speak to anyone about it, then dismissed me."

"And then what did you do?"

"I returned to my office, resumed my regular translations, which are mostly foreign news articles that have been flagged, and then finished my day, went home, spent the evening by myself at my apartment, went to sleep, then this morning came into work."

"You spoke to no one yesterday?"

"I think my mother called. Yes, my mother did call. I spoke to her for a few minutes. Other than that, it was a quiet night."

"So, you didn't mention this to anyone, friends, your father, a coworker?"

"No, sir. If you knew what the document contained, you would understand why I wouldn't dare say anything to anyone ever."

"Now you have me curious."

Victor forced a smirk. "Well, sir, I could tell you what it said, but then you'd have to kill yourself."

Nikitin tossed his head back, laughing again. "I think you're going to do well here. A sense of humor is important in this business. If you're constantly serious, eventually what you're exposed to will get to you." He indicated the door. "You're dismissed. Don't forget to report to Mr. Peskov's office. If I have any further questions for you, I know where to find you. This conversation, like that document, is classified."

Victor rose then hesitated. "Does that mean I can't talk to Mr. Peskov about what was said here?"

"There's no point in instructing you not to speak to him. And besides"—he waved a hand at the room—"I have no doubt we're being listened to. But no one else."

"Yes, sir. Understood, sir." Victor left the conference room, shaking like a leaf, and he struggled to steady his breathing as he slowly made his way to Peskov's office. So far, it appeared he had gotten away with what he did, but how long that would remain true he had no clue. Clearly, something was going on here involving the document, and even if they had no evidence he was responsible for what had happened yesterday, they might still eliminate him just to reduce the number of suspects.

He had to get out of this country. He had no choice.

It was time to reach out to the Americans.

Molly Malone's Irish Pub

Moscow, Russia

Victor stood in a corner of the packed bar, gripping an untouched glass of Baltica beer, his heart racing as the debate continued to rage in his head. He had seen something he should never have, all because of the damn job his rich father had secured him. He had to admit he had been thrilled when he landed it, and was the envy of all of his classmates. And just the mere mention of where he worked meant he rarely went home alone unless he chose to.

But yesterday, what he had been exposed to was something so terrifying in its implications, it had rocked his entire belief system to the core. He loved his country. He believed in its president. He believed in the war. Fascists who modeled themselves after the Nazis had to be destroyed. If rot like that were allowed to take hold in central Europe, there was no telling what could happen.

But while fighting fascism was a noble cause, and he couldn't understand why the West opposed it, what he had translated took things too far, and it had him rethinking things. Rethinking everything. Many of his friends had fled the country to avoid the draft, and he had dismissed the messages they had sent him claiming everything the government was telling them was a lie. His father had said it was Western hatred of Russia's success, fear of its power, that had their governments and news organizations lying about the war. But he wasn't so convinced anymore, chinks forming in the armor after what he had been reading.

The document, an agreement in principle between two allies, was terrifying. And it didn't matter who was telling the truth about the war—there was no possible good that could come of what was about to happen. And it had to be stopped, for if it wasn't, the country he loved could be destroyed. Unfortunately, there was only one way he could think of to prevent that—the secret had to come out, but he didn't know how to accomplish that. Simply posting on the Internet the photos he had taken of the document would be useless. No one would believe it, and the FSB, the federal security service, would figure out it was him within hours.

No, this wasn't something where going to the press would help, or going on social media would help. This was something that only the Americans could stop. It sickened him that he was involving his country's enemy in its internal politics, but he had no choice. If he had any doubts, the threatening conversation with Peskov after his meeting with Nikitin had convinced him he had to get himself out of the country before it was too late.

A nearby table erupted in laughter, half a dozen young American embassy staffers enjoying drinks after work on a Friday night. They were regulars here, the establishment dominated by foreigners who no longer felt comfortable at a bar filled with Russian patrons. They were the only Americans he was aware of that worked at the embassy. He would have preferred to make contact with somebody older, more mature, but he didn't hang out at bars or clubs where they did, so didn't know anybody that met the criteria. He had to settle for someone his age and pray they were smart enough to take what he gave them seriously, then have enough clout to be listened to by their superiors.

A young woman stood, grabbing her jacket off the back of her chair. "Well, I'm calling it a night. I've got some errands to run tomorrow and I don't want to do them hungover."

Victor had seen her before. She was cute, every man at her table desperate to bed her. Hell, every man in the bar and half the women were desperate to bed her. One of her colleagues, a man he recognized, rose. "I'll walk you home, Gail."

"Sure, Carl, walk her home. Is that what the kids are calling it these days?"

"You guys are pigs. You know the streets aren't safe right now, not with what happened two weeks ago." He pointed at the other men at the table. "And if I hear that you guys let any of these ladies go home alone unescorted, you'll be hearing from me on Monday."

More friendly insults were hurled, though Victor agreed with Carl's sentiment. The streets weren't as safe as they were two weeks ago, though things had vastly improved since some American named Jack had been accused of an unspeakable crime, and America and Russia had almost gone to war. He shuddered as he recalled the chatter at the office. The Americans had apparently reached DEFCON 2, one step away from all-out war.

Carl helped Gail into her jacket then put his own on, and they headed for the door. This was it. This was his chance, yet his legs refused to move. Technically, he was betraying his country. As soon as he did this, he was a traitor. And if he were found out, it meant torture, imprisonment, maybe even death. Yet was *he* the traitor? Was *he* the one betraying his country, or were those behind the scheme he had discovered the real villains here?

Perhaps it was a romanticized notion to think of himself as a hero, yet he was certain he was more hero than traitor, though both had a tendency to die in literature. He put his beer down on the ledge that circled the bar, and forced himself forward. He maneuvered through the crowd then pushed open the doors. He bundled up against the brisk cold of a Moscow winter, several inches of fresh snow covering the sidewalks from an earlier dusting. The temperature was forecast to drop rapidly overnight, and he hoped to be home before he felt its full effects.

He checked left but didn't see the two Americans, then he heard a giggle to his right. His head swung toward it and he spotted them, already a good distance ahead, his hesitancy in following them having lasted longer than he had realized. He hurried after them and quickly closed the gap, the two Americans not in any hurry, both clearly enjoying each other's company. He was certain from the way Gail was hanging on to Carl and constantly making eye contact that if Carl played his cards right, he would be getting lucky tonight. But if he were the man Victor hoped he was, any plans those two might have were about to be canceled.

They came to an intersection and the two potential lovers stopped, waiting for the crossing light to change, giving him time to reach them.

"Excuse me, Carl."

The two of them turned and Victor extended a hand, the envelope with his plea to the American government gripped tightly, the paper crinkled.

"I believe you dropped this."

Carl instinctively reached out then hesitated. "That doesn't look like mine."

You fool, haven't you been trained?

"No, it is. It came out of your pocket when you were putting on your gloves."

Carl opened his mouth again to deny it was his when Gail recognized the fear and frustration on Victor's face. She reached for it. "Oh, that's mine. Thank you so much."

Victor released his grip. He didn't care who got it as long as an American that worked at the embassy did. He turned on his heel and quickly rushed away, his heart hammering as his stomach protested. He ducked into an alleyway and vomited.

Oh, my God, what have you done?

Gail Nichols Residence

Moscow, Russia

Carl Garneau checked over his shoulder for the umpteenth time since the mysterious Russian had handed them the envelope. They had returned to Gail's apartment as casually and as calmly as they could manage, just in case they were being watched, and his paranoia was now getting the better of him.

Gail unlocked the door and pushed it aside, locking it behind them. They hurriedly stripped out of the jackets and boots, then she led them to her couch. She handed him the envelope.

"You open it."

His eyes bulged. "Me?"

"He tried to give it to you."

He frowned. "Fine." He carefully tore open the envelope and read the letter, written in English and addressed to the president of the United States, from a man named Victor Stepanov. He claimed to be a translator in the Russian president's office, and also claimed he had come across a document that could change the balance of power. He insisted it was critical America be made aware of what was happening. He was requesting asylum in America with a new identity in exchange for the document.

Carl handed it to Gail who quickly read it, her eyes widening as she read the single page.

"What do you make of it?" he asked.

"I don't know. I don't think we can ignore it."

"I guess not." He paused. "Or can we?"

She gave him a look. "You do remember orientation, don't you? We're supposed to report any contact like this immediately."

"What does immediately mean? Like Monday when we go to work?"

She shook her head. "If that's what it meant, that's what they would've said. To me, immediately means right now."

"But it's two in the morning. We're both half in the bag."

She shrugged. "I don't think that matters. It's not like we're doing anything wrong. It's Friday. We're off duty. We went to a bar. For all we know, the ambassador could be hammered."

"Please tell me you're not saying we should be calling the ambassador."

She sighed. "You really didn't pay attention during orientation, did you?"

He bristled, feeling defensive, and leaned away from her. "Of course, I paid attention. I just don't remember the exact procedure."

"We're supposed to call the switchboard and report the contact."

"Who's going to make the call?" He prayed she took the initiative. He was too drunk, and besides, it was her apartment. She rose from the couch and headed for her desk in the corner, returning with two pads of paper and pens.

"Let's write down everything that happened while it's fresh in our minds. I'm going to make some coffee."

He thanked God someone was thinking straight. He checked his phone and wrote down the date and time at the top of the page, then his name and position, cringing at how piss-poor his cursive was. He almost never wrote by hand. Everything was digital these days. He pressed the tip of the pen against the paper then paused. "Where should we start?"

Gail stopped what she was doing for a moment then resumed. "I guess from the moment we left the embassy. Actually, maybe from the moment we made plans. Whoever's reading this is going to want to figure out how this Victor guy knew where we'd be."

"Good point. It was Ian's idea, wasn't it?"

"Isn't it always?"

He chuckled. "He's always the instigator, but even if he's not at work, we still always go to the same place every Friday."

He quickly jotted down what he remembered in point form. He wasn't writing a novel. He was almost finished when Gail returned. She placed a cup of coffee in front of him.

"You take it black, right?"

He nodded and she sat beside him, jotting down her own summary, and he glanced over with envy at her flowing handwriting. "Why do girls always have such great handwriting?"

She shrugged. "I don't know. Passing a lot of notes in class?"

He frowned. "I don't think I passed a single note. I remember in high school a girl named Angela passed me a note through a friend. I can't remember what it said, but despite having a wicked crush on her, I didn't respond. I just talked to her after class. I guess I was too scared of getting in trouble."

Gail regarded him. "Only one girl ever passed you a note? A cutie like you?"

His cheeks flushed. "I was a late bloomer, I guess."

She flashed him a smile. "Well, you bloomed quite nicely."

His cheeks burned. "Thanks, but you're way hotter than I am handsome."

She leaned over and gave him a peck on the cheek. "Never use hot when describing a woman to her face."

"Pretty?"

"That's better."

"Gorgeous?"

"Ooh, even better." She resumed writing as they both downed their coffees as quickly as the temperature would permit. He reviewed his notes, inserting a few items he had forgotten, then finished his coffee.

Gail gestured toward the kitchen. "There's more."

He rose. "Refill?"

She nodded and he took her cup as well. He refilled their coffees, noting her kitchen was impeccable. He would be embarrassed to bring her back to his place, and he made a mental note to clean his apartment as soon as he returned home. Things were going well with Gail, very well, and if it weren't for this situation with the Russian and his letter, they could be burning up the sheets, starting a relationship. But that would have to wait, which meant the venue of their next encounter could change, and he didn't want to screw things up by having her think he was the slob he was.

He returned to the couch with the fresh coffees and sat beside her, a little closer than when he had left.

She handed him her pad. "You want to read this over, see if I forgot anything?"

He took it and handed her his own. He reviewed her statement, the handwriting beautiful. He couldn't remember the last time he had read something handwritten, and it reminded him of middle school and a girl named Thea that he had been crushing hard on. She had been the first girl to ever stroke his inner thigh in a suggestive manner. Unfortunately, she had done it in the middle of English class, much too close to the bell, leaving him gripping his binder against a rager, but forever in love with the touch of a woman.

Her handwriting had been exquisite as well, and she had this unique way of writing the letter T where she didn't lift her pen to cross them. He had emulated her for a brief while until she broke his heart, turning her attentions to a mullet-sporting boy nicknamed Ace.

Tragic.

He finished reading Gail's statement, far more thorough than his, as she had gone with a narrative rather than point form. He looked up to see her smiling at him.

"Where were you?"

"Huh?"

"At one point you weren't reading. Your eyes stopped moving. It's like you were lost in thought."

His cheeks burned once again. "Umm, middle school."

She faced him, curling her leg up under her knee. "Oh? What was her name?"

His eyes drifted to the floor. "Thea."

"Sexy."

"She's nothing compared to you."

"I should hope not, if she was in middle school."

He laughed. "You know what I mean."

She patted his cheek. "I wish my name was Thea. Much sexier."

"Trust me, there's no one sexier than you."

She leaned in, pressing her forehead against his and closing her eyes. "Oh, you were going to get so lucky tonight." She sighed heavily then pulled away, tapping her notepad. "Unfortunately, we've got a phone call to make first."

He groaned as he leaned back, but not before reaching out and taking her hand and clasping it to his chest. He stared into her eyes. "Please tell me we'll get a second chance at this."

She grinned. "Who knows? They might not want to see us until the morning."

69

He bolted upright. "Then let's make that damn call!"

She giggled and grabbed him by the back of the head, drawing him in and kissing him, a long slow tender kiss that left no doubt in his mind that she was as interested as he was, and his heart fluttered with the thought that this could be his last first kiss.

Chief of Station's Office, Embassy of the United States

Moscow, Russia

Carl struggled to control his racing heart and Gail reached out, taking his hand and giving it a comforting squeeze. He smiled weakly at her then rapidly let go when there was a noise at the door. They were sitting in the outer office of the Chief of Station, waiting for her to arrive, and this could be her.

Gail had made the call, since it was her apartment. She had given the code word indicating a foreign contact, and they were ordered in immediately, a car from the embassy picking them up fifteen minutes later. When they had arrived, they had met with the duty officer who read the letter, read their statements, then called in the Chief of Station.

And they had been waiting since, slowly sobering up.

The door opened and Moscow Chief of Station Patricia Arbuckle entered wearing casual clothes and a yawn. Carl leaped to his feet, Gail a split second behind him. "Good morning, ma'am," they both echoed.

Arbuckle waved them off as she unlocked her inner office, beckoning them to follow. "Sit. It's too early in the morning for formalities." She dropped in her chair, placing a large thermos on the desktop along with a file folder sporting a classified tag. "How drunk are you two?"

"Fairly," replied Carl as Gail contradicted him.

"Not very."

They both exchanged nervous glances.

"Well, which is it?"

Gail leaned forward. "I wouldn't drive, but I only had a few drinks. I have plans in the morning."

Arbuckle redirected her focus to Carl. "And you?"

"Half a dozen beers maybe. I definitely wouldn't drive and I certainly wouldn't come into work. If you're asking if I'm floor-licking pissed, then no. I'm not slurring my words." He suddenly doubted himself and his head spun toward Gail. "I'm not, am I?"

"No, you're not."

"Good," said Arbuckle. "Then we'll begin informally. In the morning things will really get going when you're both legally sober." She shook the file folder. "I've read your statements. Good thinking, by the way."

Carl jerked a thumb at Gail. "That was her idea."

"Well, it was a good one. Record everything while things are still fresh. Now, about this letter—"

"Do you think it's serious?" asked Gail.

Arbuckle regarded her. "Would I be here at this ungodly hour if I didn't?"

Gail leaned back, staring at her hands. "Sorry."

Carl leaped to her defense, perhaps a little too quickly. "I think it's a reasonable question."

Arbuckle poured what turned out to be coffee from the thermos, filling her mug that sat on her desk, the side of it emblazoned with MFWIC, and Carl wondered what the acronym meant. The inebriated part of his brain wanted to ask, but thankfully it had minimal control right now.

She tapped the file. "In your statement, Carl, you said you recognized him."

"Yes, I've seen him at the bar before."

"Have you ever spoken to him?"

He shrugged. "I don't think so. Certainly never had a conversation with him. Might have said hello or something like that if we bumped into each other in the crowd."

"So, you've never formally met Victor Stepanov?"

"No, definitely not." His eyes narrowed. "Why? Have I?"

"I'd be stunned if you did." Arbuckle opened the file folder and leafed through several pages before lifting a photo of the man who had handed them the letter. "Is this him?"

They both nodded. "Yeah, that's him," said Gail. She squinted. "Why do we have a file on him?"

"Because his father is very high profile. Have you ever heard of Alexei Stepanov?"

Head shakes.

"Well, he's a Russian oligarch. Mining. And a huge supporter of the Russian president. So, naturally, we keep tabs on him and his family." She tapped the photo. "This is his son who recently started his career as a translator in the Russian president's office."

Carl's eyes shot wide. "Holy shit, so then this is legit?"

"It could be, and it's the only reason why I'm here at this hour. When the son of one of Russia's wealthiest men, whose family is a staunch supporter of the Russian president, and who actually works in the president's office, claims to have valuable intelligence and is essentially requesting to defect, it gets my attention." She again held up the photo. "And you're positive this was him, not just someone who looks like him?"

Carl hesitated. It had been dark. The man had his hood up, covering some of his features. "I'm pretty sure. I mean, looking at him, it does look like the guy, doesn't it?" he asked, turning to Gail.

She shifted in her chair. "I think it is. But am I one hundred percent positive? No. It was nighttime. We were a little drunk and it was cold out, so he had his hood up. He didn't have a scarf on or anything like that, but it certainly looked like him. And the fact that his name matches the letter, doesn't that kind of mean it is him?"

Arbuckle firmly dismissed the assertion. "No, it doesn't. The FSB could have had somebody who looked like him play the part to trick us. We'd go through a song and dance, get our hands on this intel, it would turn out to be false, but we'd waste days, weeks, or maybe even months figuring that out. It's a game both sides play. You're always trying to hand the other guy garbage just so that the one time it's real, it has them doubting it, hopefully long enough to mitigate the leak."

"You mean we could be getting played?" asked Carl. The idea pissed him off. Right now, he should be making love to Gail, instead he was here at work on a Friday night, rather than sealing the deal with a woman he had been infatuated with for months.

"Yes, but I don't think that's what's happening in this case."

"Why not?" asked Gail.

"The FSB would never use so high profile a person to impersonate. They would use a nobody. The fact this letter claims to have been written by Victor Stepanov, I have to assume this is genuine, and act accordingly."

"What do you think this document he claims to have come across deals with?"

"No idea. However, with the current state of affairs between Russia and our country, and much of the world for that matter, there's a very good chance it actually is something critical, as opposed to the exaggeration of somebody who's just trying to escape the draft."

Carl grunted. "Something tells me with his father, he doesn't have to worry about that. Little rich kids rarely have to live in the reality the rest of us do."

Arbuckle regarded him. "Do I detect a hint of bitterness?"

Carl dismissed the question with a wave of his hand. "Sorry, ignore me. My filter is faulty right now." Unfortunately, his filter failed him again. "It's just that I had to work for everything I have. My parents couldn't afford to put me through college, so I worked my ass off washing dishes, busing tables for four years. Then I had to compete to get my first government job and work my ass off to be able to get a foreign posting. My father was a long-haul trucker. Nobody ever gave him anything and nobody ever gave me anything. If my dad tried to make a call to get me a job, whatever senator or rep that claimed to be looking out for us wouldn't have given him the time of day."

"Is this going to be a problem for you?"

Carl regarded the woman, already regretting what he had said. "No. What does it matter? It's not like we're involved anymore."

"Oh, you're definitely still involved."

Carl's stomach flipped. "Why's that?"

"Because, according to both your statements, our rich boy tried to give you the envelope."

En route to Chkalovsky Air Base

Moscow, Russia

Kane cleared the checkpoint on the outskirts of Moscow, his forged documents provided by Moscow Station passing muster as expected. Langley had him on what might potentially be a wild goose chase, though that didn't mean it was no less dangerous. After the incident at Peskov's residence, the NSA had detected a flurry of communications between the Russian president's office and eight different military facilities across the country. He was headed to one of them, Chkalovsky Air Base, where one of the communications had gone out to. It was a known home of the Kh-47M2 Kinzhal hypersonic missile, a missile designed to be attached to a fighter jet and dropped from high altitude where it would then reach speeds of up to Mach 5 as it descended toward its target, almost unstoppable, though every time the Russians used one in Ukraine, NATO collected more data, and he had no doubt weapons designers the world over were working on an effective countermeasure.

But that could be years in the offing.

If he could get evidence that there were Kinzhal, or "Dagger" missiles ready for shipment, as opposed to launch, it could at least confirm what the Russians were selling the Chinese. Right now, he was Captain Maxim Mironov, assigned to the post. The real Captain Mironov, whose face had been copied by Moscow Station, was passed out in a cheap hotel room, surrounded by photos of him doing unspeakable things with a prostitute named Olga, and a note.

Don't report for work until tomorrow.

Mironov had a known drug problem and it wouldn't be the first time he missed a day of work, though someone always took his place, and today that was Kane. Setting the poor bastard up had taken a full day, leaving Kane to twiddle his thumbs most of yesterday at the safe house until a good friend had arrived that had helped kill the time.

But he was eager to be back in the game.

Mironov's car reeked of air fresheners, no doubt to cover up the stench of the meth smoked inside it on occasion, but it solidified his cover. It didn't take long to reach the base on the outskirts of Moscow, and he was quickly cleared through with knowing frowns by those who regularly manned the front gate, no doubt unimpressed they wore the same uniform. But it was perfect. The fewer words exchanged, the less familiarity shown, the better.

Since Mironov had been used before, they knew a lot about him, including where his office was, an office he manned alone, and a position that gave him free rein of the base. His orders from Langley were to hole up in the office and wait for nightfall, then take a tour of the hardened storage facilities to see what he could find. He intended to catch up on his sleep, and if he were caught in such a compromising position, he would be 100% in character.

He just wondered which straw would break the camel's back and have poor Captain Mironov, victim of the pipe, transferred to the front.

Molly Malone's Irish Pub
Moscow, Russia

"You have to relax, sweetie. You're even making me nervous."

CIA Operations Officer Sherrie White stood in the corner of the Irish pub, a quintessentially Irish AK-47 sitting on a nearby table. Langley had sent her in yesterday. She had only been back stateside less than a week after the events involving Jack. Her poor boyfriend, CIA Analyst Supervisor Chris Leroux, was probably thankful for the break. With everything she had gone through in those couple of days, she had come home with an insatiable sexual appetite that demanded satisfaction, and he had paid the exquisite price.

When she had been briefed about the op, it sounded rather routine except for who was involved, and she had to agree it needed to be taken seriously. And while she would have loved to stay at home for another week, recovering from her bumps and bruises and the most stressful situation she had ever been in in her life, she loved her job and couldn't imagine doing anything else. But it wasn't for everyone. Through the course of her brief career, she had been beaten, stabbed, shot, and blown up, with the scars to prove it. But she wouldn't change a thing. Well, perhaps she would have chosen not to be shot. Or stabbed or beaten for that matter. And if the rank amateur she was working with didn't settle down, if this were a setup, the no doubt experienced FSB agents in the room would identify her and pick her up for interrogation despite all she had done for their country two short weeks ago.

"Just relax, it'll be fine."

Carl glanced over at her and she cursed.

"Don't look at me!"

His head quickly jerked away and she rolled her eyes.

This better not be a setup.

An embassy worker, properly trained and part of Moscow Station, had bumped into Victor on his way leaving work earlier today, a message whispered in his ear.

9:00 PM at the bar.

She resisted the urge to check her watch, and instead took a drink, using the glass to hide her mouth. "Time check."

"8:59. Still no sign of him," replied the love of her life in her ear, Control Actual for the op.

He better show.

She was dying to know what the intel was. The eldest child of one of the most powerful families in Russia, who just so happened to work in the Russian president's office, had to have found something juicy if he were demanding asylum. To walk away from billions was a decision she hoped she could make if she were put in the same situation he apparently was.

But this could all be bullshit.

"Stand by, Skylark. We've got eyes on the target."

She breathed a sigh of relief and raised her glass, bringing her CIA-customized Ballon Blue de Cartier watch near her mouth, the device paired to the earpiece tucked deep within Carl's ear canal. "Victor's on his way in."

Carl flinched but said nothing, instead resuming what appeared to be an awkward conversation with Gail.

"He's entering now," reported Leroux.

Sherrie casually glanced over to see Victor step inside the bar, white as a ghost, his eyes wide. He scanned the room and she averted his gaze. His search ended the moment he spotted Carl and Gail sitting at their table. She pushed off the wall and headed for him, her form-hugging outfit accentuating all of her assets. She smiled at him as her finger traced the lip of her glass. "Can I buy you a drink?"

"No, I'm meeting someone."

"Actually, you're meeting me."

He flinched, staring at her. "I don't understand."

"I work with your friends at that table over there. Come sit with me at the bar and have a drink so that we don't draw attention."

He shook out an uncertain nod then followed her. She held up her glass. "Can I get another Stoli on the rocks?" She turned to Victor. "What would you like?"

"The same, I guess."

"Two Stolis coming up," said the bartender.

Sherrie leaned forward and stroked Victor's outer thigh as if she were hitting on him. "Just relax. We want everyone to think we're two potential lovers getting to know each other."

He gulped. "All right. Wh-what happens now?"

"We're going to have our drink, then we're going to leave. We're going to get in a cab, then go somewhere safe and talk."

"How do I know I can trust you?"

She smiled. "You trusted them."

"I had no choice. I didn't know who else might be able to help. How do I know you actually work with them?"

"Watch." Their drinks were delivered and Sherrie picked up her glass, raising it to her mouth. "I want you to both raise your glasses and clink them together, then put them down without taking a drink."

She didn't bother looking, Victor's bulging eyes confirming her instructions had been followed to the letter.

"How?"

She smiled. "Does it matter? Now you know that I'm with them. If you trusted them, you have to trust me. They're nobodies. They don't have the power to get you what you want."

"And you do?"

"Let's just say I'm many steps closer to the people who can. They sent me, and depending on what you have to offer, we can make a deal tonight."

Victor reached for his drink, his hand trembling.

"Take a deep breath and slowly let it out."

He sniffed hard and exhaled rapidly, making things worse.

She reached out and squeezed his thigh. "Slowly. Calm down. Now have a drink. It'll settle your nerves."

He inhaled again, this time following her instructions, then exhaled. And downed half his drink.

"Good." She reached out and stroked his cheek and he drained his glass. She took his hand. "How about we get out of here and go back to my place," she said, her voice a little louder.

He nodded.

"Now pay for our drinks."

He stared at her wide-eyed. "But I thought you said you were buying me a drink?"

"But you're a gentleman, aren't you?"

He fished out his wallet and stuck a wad of rubles underneath his empty glass. He stepped off his stool and she extended her arms. He helped her off hers then they headed for the door and retrieved their jackets. He helped her into hers then they stepped into the frigid cold. She wrapped herself around his arm as a cab parked just down the street, its roof light off, pulled away from the curb. Its light flickered on and she raised her hand, the car pulling up beside them. She climbed in, Victor following, and their CIA driver pulled away, keeping a watchful eye out for any tail.

"Are we clear?" she asked.

"Yeah, doesn't look like anyone's following us, but that doesn't mean we're clear. We could have a drone parked right overhead."

She activated her comms. "Control, Skylark, any sign they're following us?"

"Negative, Skylark, it looks clear. No sign of any drones or tail cars."

"Good. Tell our two helpers to stick around for ten minutes before they leave."

"Roger that."

"I'll contact you at the safe house. Skylark, out." She turned in her seat to face Victor. "Okay, we're safe in here. This is an embassy car. Now, do you have the intel with you?"

Victor opened his mouth to reply then thought better of it, his jaw snapping shut. He sniffed hard then held his breath for a moment before replying. "I need to know, can you get me out?"

"*Can* we get you out? Absolutely. *Will* we get you out depends on what it is you have to offer."

"No, that's not the deal. Even if you don't like what I have to offer, you have to get me out. I won't be safe."

Sherrie frowned. "Listen, that's not the way it works. You have to—"

Victor cut her off, jabbing a finger at her. "No, I don't care how you think it works. Do you have any idea who I am? Who my family is? Where I work? I'm giving up everything to do the right thing. All I ask in return is that you get me safely to America with a new identity. You guys do this all the time, I'm sure. I just want out, because once I tell you what I found out and you act on it, it won't take them long to figure out who the leak was. I…" His voice cracked and his eyes pooled with tears as his head dropped to his chest. "I don't want to die, and I definitely don't want to be tortured if they catch me."

God only knew what they would do to him despite who his father was. Sherrie felt for the young man, but her feelings were irrelevant. All that mattered was whether she believed he was telling the truth, and she certainly believed he believed. The question was whether what he believed was reality. He thought he had a critical piece of intel, but it might be worthless. It could be false. It could be unimportant. It could be something they were already fully aware of. Just because some 22-year-old kid thought he had discovered some bombshell that would change the world, didn't make it so.

But he was right about one thing, and that was the fact that they did this all the time. The expense of extracting him and giving him a new identity was minimal.

"Listen," she said, her voice gentle as she took his hand, clasping it in both of hers. "Convince me. My recommendation carries a lot of weight. Tell me what the intel has to deal with. You don't need to show it to me. Just tell me, and if I like what I hear, I'll get the ball rolling."

"I don't know."

She took a chance. "Listen, we know it involves hypersonic missiles."

Victor's eyes shot wide and he vehemently shook his head. "No, that's not at all what they're selling. They're selling something far worse."

Chkalovsky Air Base
Outside Moscow, Russia

Kane activated his comms as he strode toward the storage area, bundled up in winter dress, the Russian idea of warmth for its troops falling far shy of the American definition. "Control, Wild One. What have you got for me?"

Leroux replied, his team monitoring the base all day. If there were a shipment of hypersonic missiles within one of the structures ahead, the security would either be tight or almost non-existent, so as not to draw attention. At a minimum, there would be little activity going in and out, not only due to the nature of the weapons, but also the fact that they should be prepped for shipping, not immediate deployment. "We've actually been able to eliminate most of the buildings. There's just too much activity going in and out of most of them. We've narrowed it down to a cluster of six at the far end of the field. Nobody's gone in or out of them all day, and they're close to the railroad tracks, if that's how they're going to transport them."

"Security?"

"Minimal. Two foot patrols, one with a dog."

"Where are they now?"

"We're designating the team with the dog as Team One. They should be at your two o'clock, heading away from you."

Kane spotted them. "And Team Two?"

"On the opposite side of the block of buildings. It looks like they're just doing the perimeter repeatedly. There are no footprints in the snow indicating they're going up and down between the buildings, or even checking any of the doors."

Kane spotted the group of six buildings as he passed a large hangar containing half a dozen Sukhoi fighter jets. He made a beeline for the building on the far right, closest to the fence. "I'm designating them buildings one to six, from left to right. Heading for Building Six now. Entrances?"

"Well, you've got that big door in the front."

Kane chuckled at Leroux's reference to the door stretching across most of the building. "Yeah, I think they might notice."

"There's an access door on the front-right."

Kane dismissed the idea. "Too in the open. What's on the sides or the back?"

"The back has more large doors that give them access to the rail line. Each side has a single door that you should be able to access. I can't tell you if they're alarmed, though."

"Copy that. I'm going to try the door on the number four side." He continued his brisk walk, timing his arrival at the corner of the building to coincide with Team One's rounding to the back. He waited for the all-clear from Leroux then continued, making certain to remain in the footprints already laid until he arrived at the door. He fished out his phone, the customized device already scanning for signals. He ran it around the door frame and detected one, likely a wireless sensor that would transmit an alarm to a central monitoring station when the circuit was broken. A few taps on his screen had the signal cloned, then he placed a highly localized jamming device where the sensor was, and activated it. It would scramble the sensor, but his phone should continue transmitting the signal if all went according to plan.

He listened for any indicators that something had fouled up, but heard nothing. "I've overridden the door sensor. Any sign they've noticed anything?"

"Negative."

He removed his lock pick gun from his pocket and shoved it in the door lock, squeezing it several times. He tried the handle and the door opened. He pushed on it gently, opening it a sliver, and spotted the sensor. He reached into his pocket and pulled out his wallet. He retrieved what appeared to be a Magnit loyalty card. He peeled off a strip of plastic from the back, exposing an adhesive strip, then pressed the card over the sensor, bridging the signal. He deactivated the jammer then stared at the display on his phone.

Success.

No change in the signal. He removed the jammer, gently closed the door, then removed the credit card. He peered into the inky blackness, the only light in the entire large hardened warehouse coming from lone bulbs over each of the four exits, their red hue not carrying far.

"Control, Wild One. I'm in. Am I still secure?"

"As far as we can tell, but whatever you do, you better hurry. Team Two is at the front of the block now."

"I'm not worried about them. I'm worried about the one with the dog. Just a second. I'm going to shed some light on the situation." He activated the flashlight function on his phone and played it around. Directly in front of him was a large shipping container. He quickly strode to the end of it, playing his light around the corner, revealing a long line of matching containers reaching all the way to the far end. "I'm counting six shipping containers," he reported. "No sign of any missiles. I'm going to have to open one of them."

"Copy that, Wild One."

He ran his phone as best he could around the back of the container he stood in front of and along the door-locking mechanism, but found nothing indicating it was wired. In fact, the lock on the seal remained open. The Russians were obviously confident in their security and would only lock the container when it was leaving.

Or there was nothing inside to protect.

He opened the seal and swung the right side of the container door aside, cringing as the hinges creaked. He steadied the door so it didn't swing on its own, then peered into the darkness. There was something there. What, he couldn't tell. He pulled his phone out of his pocket, the flashlight still shining, and held it up.

And gasped. "Holy shit!"

"What?" asked a concerned Leroux in his ear.

"You're not going to believe this." He quickly started snapping photos, automatically transmitting them to Langley.

"Oh, my God!" exclaimed Leroux, obviously having received at least the first photo. "This can't be right."

Operations Center 3, CIA Headquarters

Langley, Virginia

Leroux stared at the image on the massive display that arced across the front of the operation center. "Please tell me that isn't what I think it is."

Tong stared, her mouth agape. "I wish I could." She spun in her chair, pointing at Marc Therrien. "Run it. We need to know for sure."

"Yes, ma'am." Therrien attacked his keyboard, another window opening on the display, the computer enhancing the image, detecting the edges, a wireframe rapidly constructed of what was the front of a large truck, its distinct design obvious to anyone familiar with Russian and Soviet-era hardware. The computer raced through its database, quickly finding a match, the results they all feared showing on the screen.

It was a Russian RS-24 Yars mobile MIRV-equipped ICBM system.

Tong turned to Leroux. "Are we seriously saying that the Russians are actually selling these things to the Chinese?"

Leroux's head slowly shook in disbelief. "It could be coincidence, I suppose. But why would they have them prepped for transport just like Peskov said they would?"

Child spun in his chair. "Isn't this illegal? I mean, doesn't it violate all kinds of international treaties?"

Leroux grunted. "I think it violates them all. If Washington wants to go public with this, we're going to need more proof than just some photos. For all we know, they're prepping to redeploy them to another part of their own country. One of the other buildings might have been loaded with hypersonic missiles." He turned to Danny Packman. "Start pulling satellite footage we have of that facility. Work your way back. I want to see if we can spot these things arriving."

"They might have brought them in on containers just to keep prying eyes like ours off them."

"Let's just look for anything going in and out of those buildings."

"Yes, sir."

Leroux flipped his comms over to Sherrie's frequency. "Skylark, Control Actual, come in, over."

"Control, Skylark, you're not going to believe what Victor just said they're selling to the Chinese. He says it's not hypersonic missiles. It's the bulk of the Russian nuclear arsenal."

Leroux's chest tightened with Sherrie's report, the deal apparently going far beyond fifty mobile platforms. "We've just confirmed what your asset said. We need to get him secure, stat, and we need that intel. No more bullshit. But get yourself secure first, over."

"Roger that, Control. Heading to the safe house now. Skylark, out."

Leroux flipped back to Kane. "Wild One, Control Actual. We need to get as much proof as we can of this. Our Russian contact has confirmed that this is what's for sale, not hypersonic missiles."

"Understood, Control. Working on it."

Chkalovsky Air Base

Outside Moscow, Russia

Kane hurried down to the next container and opened it, finding the same inside. He took more photos. "I've just confirmed there's more than one. That's the second container."

"Can you confirm they're real? They're not just mock-ups?"

Kane reached forward and rapped his knuckles against the metal. "Oh, these things are real. There's no doubt about it. I think we've just stumbled upon the biggest arms deal in the history of the world."

"And the most dangerous," agreed Leroux. "What do you want to do?"

Kane stared at the ominous sight in front of him, a Russian RS-24 Yars, a mobile weapons system on wheels, as comfortable on the roads as a semi. It was an Intercontinental Ballistic Missile launcher with requisite missile, no doubt equipped with Multiple Independently-targetable Reentry Vehicles including six nuclear warheads capable of hitting targets pretty much anywhere in the world. It could easily move about the countryside, hardened silos not required, meaning you never knew where they were to take them out before they could be launched. This was a game-changer. Hypersonic missiles were one thing. They were conventional. They could cause a lot of damage, but that damage was restricted. These were nuclear, and they weren't even tactical—they were strategic. These were designed to take out military bases, cities, fleets. They were an offensive weapon meant to give the Russians an edge in any nuclear exchange, and they were selling them to the Chinese.

He made a decision.

He retrieved his wallet again, peeling back the inner layer of the billfold, revealing six small round discs. He pulled one out and dropped to a knee, attaching the magnetic device underneath the bumper and out of sight. "Activate tracker number one."

"Activating. Signal confirmed. Our specs show there should be serial numbers for each unit on the right rear quarter panel."

"Just a second." Kane squeezed between the massive vehicle and the container wall. Scurrying to the far end of the container, he found the panel and took several photos. "Got it."

"Can you confirm it has a missile?"

"Absolutely," replied Kane, staring up at the terrifying cylinder. He brought up another app on his phone, activating a radiological scanner, confirming what he already knew. "I'm showing much more than background radiation here. This thing has at least one warhead on it."

"Understood. Your guards are coming to the number four side now. Suggest you wrap things up. I think we've got our proof."

"Yeah, I think so." Kane slithered back down the side of the container then resealed it. He placed a tag on the first two missile systems then headed for the door.

"Stand by, Wild One." Leroux cursed. "They've taken an interest in the door."

"They must have spotted my footprints."

"Team One is now running to the front of the building. That dog's going to pick up your scent the moment he reaches the opposite corner."

"Copy that." Kane sprinted toward the door at the opposite side of the building. He jammed his credit card between the sensor and the door then opened it up, glancing at his phone to make sure no emergency signal had been sent. He pressed the micro jammer into the doorframe and activated it, his phone taking over, sending a clear signal. Everything still looked good.

"They're all at the door now."

"Do they have a key?" he asked as he gently closed the door then removed the credit card.

"It doesn't appear so. One of them is on his radio."

Kane removed the jammer, deactivating it, and checked again to confirm there was no indication he had tripped the alarm. He reached into his pocket and pulled out a pack of cigarettes he had taken from Mironov's office. He tore half of it off, stuffing it back in his pocket, then lit the other half. He took a couple of drags then tossed it in front of the door, still lit, then raced down the side of the building.

"We've got a security vehicle coming. You should see it now," reported Leroux.

Kane hugged the corner of the building and spotted the vehicle in question as it raced toward the structure, its lights flickering in the dark. It skidded to a halt at the opposite corner, the two men inside jumping out and disappearing around the side.

And he made a decision that could either mean his life or his freedom. "Tell Fang I love her."

Leroux groaned in his ear as Kane jogged along the front of the building, heading for the security teams. "What the hell are you doing?"

"About the only damn thing I can do." He lit another cigarette on the run, then rounded the corner, hailing the six men and one dog. "Do we have a problem here?" The men all spun toward him, weapons raised, the dog snarling and pulling against its leash.

"Identify yourself!"

"Captain Mironov."

"I hope you know what you're doing," muttered Leroux.

"Me too." He held up a hand, shielding his eyes from the flashlights now aimed at him. He tapped his rank insignia. "Lower those lights. Who's in charge?"

A sergeant stepped forward. "I am, sir. Sergeant Oreshkin."

"Report."

"One of our patrols spotted footprints near the doorway here."

Kane stepped over and leaned in, then laughed. He shoved his own boot into the snow beside the stray print. "It's mine."

"Sir, what business did you have here?"

"None." Kane held up the cigarette. "I was trying to light my cigarette so I ducked into the doorway here to block the wind."

The sergeant eyed him suspiciously before pointing at the impressions in the snow encircling the building. "Then why did you try to hide your footprints?"

"What the hell are you talking about, Sergeant?"

The sergeant pointed. "That's the only footprint of yours I see. That means you walked inside the patrol's footprints. Why would you do that?"

Kane rolled his eyes. "Sergeant, when's the last time you were on foot patrol in heavy snow?"

"Sir?"

Kane flicked his cigarette, the ash dropping into the snow as he gestured at the two teams actually on patrol. "Why don't you ask them why I used their footprints?"

The sergeant still stared at him, but a young corporal leaned forward. "Because it's easier, sir."

The sergeant's eyes darted toward the younger man then he cursed. "Fine. But, Captain, I need to ask what your business here is."

"Nothing. I'm in the middle of a long boring shift and I'm out for a cigarette break."

"But why are you at this end of the base?"

"I'm cleared for every area. And when I'm on one of my smoke breaks, I have absolutely no interest in talking to anybody, so I go where nobody is."

"Can I see your identification, sir?"

Kane handed it over and the sergeant inspected it with his flashlight. "Oh, Captain Mironov."

It was said as if he knew exactly who the infamous captain was. "Yes?"

"Nothing, sir." He handed the ID back. "You're free to go, but I'll have to ask that you avoid this end of the base for the next two days unless it's official business."

Kane returned his ID to his pocket, deciding to fish a little. "What happens in two days?"

The sergeant shrugged. "No idea. All I know is our extra security patrols are scheduled to be finished at that point."

"Understood, Sergeant." Kane turned to the four men making up the patrols. "And gentlemen, excellent job. With men like you guarding our facility, the Ukrainians and Americans have no hope in hell of breaching our security."

All four snapped to attention. "Thank you, sir!" they replied in unison.

The sergeant followed by the rest saluted and Kane returned the gesture before heading back to the road, the sergeant and his partner following. "Can we offer you a ride, sir?"

Kane held up his cigarette. "I'm not done. You go ahead. There's nothing I enjoy more than a crisp Moscow night." He passed their vehicle and they climbed in as he continued nonchalantly back to his office. "Report."

Leroux sighed in his ear. "Patrols have resumed. It looks like you got away with it, at least for now."

"And those trackers?"

"Strong signals from all three. We should be able to tell where they end up heading."

Kane tossed his cigarette in the snow. "Oh, I think we know exactly where they're heading. The question is, are we going to stop them?"

Operations Center 3, CIA Headquarters

Langley, Virginia

Leroux rose, snapping his fingers at the room. "I want everyone on this. If this is true, this is enormous. We have to secure that intel. And if the Russians have even caught wind of the leak, you know they're going to be all over it." He turned to his second-in-command, Sonya Tong. "I have to go brief the Chief, so I'm leaving this with you. Watch for tails, drones, hacks on cameras along their route, satellite re-taskings. Monitor all their frequencies. Anything you can think of. And notify Chief of Station Moscow that this could be legit and to take all necessary precautions. I highly recommend they get their two employees on a plane back to the States pronto, because when Victor doesn't show up for work tomorrow, they're going to start backtracking his movements. And start working out a way to discreetly contact his father. Once we have Victor safely out of the country, his family might want extraction as well, because somebody's going to be blamed for this."

"I'm on it," replied Tong as Leroux passed through the double set of doors designed to block any stray signals from getting in or out, then headed for the elevators. If what Kane had just found, and Victor had just told Sherrie, was true, the implications were staggering. If they couldn't stop what was about to happen, the balance of power could shift dramatically, creating a new Asian power block that the United States would have no hope of countering.

He couldn't believe the Russians would consider such a thing. It couldn't possibly be true. It was illegal on so many levels, violated international treaties, international law, and it was so dangerous that he couldn't believe anyone would risk it. Yet the Russians had shown time and again that treaties meant nothing to them, that the rule of law was something they laughed at, and that putting the world at risk wasn't even a second thought if they believed it could benefit their country.

He emerged from the elevators and jogged to the end of the hall. He cleared security to the executive offices, and as he entered Morrison's outer office, he pointed at the door. "Is he in?"

Morrison's assistant tapped the intercom. "Chris Leroux to see you, sir." She nodded toward the door. "He'll see you now."

Leroux entered to find National Clandestine Service Chief Leif Morrison sitting at his desk, staring at a computer screen. He looked up.

"I take it you've got an update on the Moscow operation?"

Leroux dropped in a chair in front of the Chief's desk. "Yes, sir. And you're not going to believe what we just found out."

103

Morrison leaned forward, and when Leroux told him, his hand snapped out, grabbing his phone. "Get me the president."

CIA Safe House
Moscow, Russia

Sherrie waited for the garage door to roll closed before stepping out of their fake cab. Their driver climbed out then headed for the door to the inside of the house. He tapped in a 2-1-2 pattern and glanced up at a camera mounted above.

"Charlie-Charlie-four-seven-two-three-Alpha. I've got two guests." There was a buzz then a click, and he pushed open the door. "Let's go," he said, beckoning Sherrie and Victor inside.

Victor tentatively followed as Sherrie brought up the rear, as tense as she ever had been. The idea the Russians were selling their nuclear arsenal to China was unthinkable, yet as they had driven here in silence, she had come to realize it made perfect sense. The Chinese had money to burn and could easily afford to pay an exorbitant price for the weapon systems, and could also afford to maintain them, something the Russians couldn't anymore.

The deal would catapult the Chinese nuclear weapons program ahead overnight. It was suspected that the Chinese had several hundred warheads. It was a respectable deterrent, though if all-out war were to occur, America could pummel them back into the Stone Age. But if they suddenly had hundreds of additional missiles, perhaps even thousands, depending on the extent of this deal, they would never worry about America again interfering in its affairs. The Russians would get massive cash infusions for every weapon sold, plus save billions a year in no longer having to maintain the extremely dangerous devices.

She stepped inside the CIA safe house where she was greeted by two armed guards in civilian clothes. One of them smiled at her. "No point giving you some bullshit name. You can call me Jane." She jerked a thumb at her partner. "This is Larry."

Larry waved with a smile. "Any idea how long you're going to be here?"

Sherrie shook her head. "Hopefully not long. I'm just waiting to hear back from Langley on getting him into the underground railroad." She turned to Victor. "They're going to want that intel."

"Not until I'm safe."

She cursed. "You know what we're dealing with here." She held up a finger, warning him off. "Don't say anything in front of anyone. They're not cleared for this intel, but you know how serious this is. We've just confirmed that you're telling the truth, but we need the paperwork."

"And you'll have it when I'm safe."

Larry jerked a thumb over his shoulder at a nearby door. "We have a beating room in the basement if you need it."

Victor's eyebrows shot up. "Did he say beating or meeting?"

Larry grinned. "I don't see anyone in a suit around here."

CIA Safe House

Moscow, Russia

Kane turned the water off to the shower, running his hands over his naked body, wiping away the beaded water before stepping out and snatching a towel. He dried off as the fan hummed, doing its job ineffectually as the mirror was fogged up. He had stuck around the base for another half-hour then left, feigning illness, before joining Sherrie and their guest. There was still no indication of any concern from the installation, and it appeared he had gotten away with his exploration.

In the two hours that had passed, he had had plenty of time to think, and he wasn't certain how to proceed. The president was being briefed on what had been discovered, but they still didn't have the actual intel from Victor, and it was key. Without it, all they had were photos of a weapon system everyone knew the Russians owned. There was no proof that anything was being sold to the Chinese in violation of countless treaties.

They needed the paperwork.

He toweled off then opened the door, stepping into the bedroom he had been assigned in the safe house. Sherrie squealed in delight from her perch on the bed. "Ooh, nobody told me it was your birthday."

He laughed, not bothering to cover up, modesty between two officers who often had to play lovers completely unnecessary. "Any luck with our Russian friend?"

"Still refuses to speak. He's terrified."

He pulled on a pair of underwear.

"Aww!"

He gave her a look then returned to business. "I can understand why. Hypersonic missiles are one thing, but nuclear missiles, that's something entirely different. One's just a straight high-tech weapons deal. The other is criminal and potentially extremely deadly. That's probably why they're trying to transfer as many systems as they can as quickly as they can. If the Chinese have fifty of these in the next week, even if the deal is stopped, it'll still be worth their while and they can give us the middle finger until the cows come home. Remember, it's fifty missiles, but it's three hundred warheads. They know there's nothing we'll do about it beyond economic sanctions, which will hurt us just as much as them since we hooked our wagon to their manufacturing base years ago. They can move on Taiwan as soon as they're ready to, and simply threaten nuclear retaliation if we interfere."

"Do you think it would come to that? Do you think they would actually nuke us?"

"No, not unless we went into all-out war. They wouldn't nuke us, they'd nuke Taiwan because they know we wouldn't respond. No American president is going to risk nuclear war over a foreign country unless it were a NATO member, and even then I wouldn't be so sure. And the Chinese know it. The more of these weapons they get into their hands before we can stop it, the more secure they become from any threat of interference by us. The Russians will still have plenty of missiles to defend themselves, and they probably have some sort of mutual defense pact as part of the deal. And with the money they'll receive over the long term, they'll be able to counteract any of the sanctions we currently have against them."

"If we get the proof, what do you think the president will do?"

Kane shrugged as he sat beside her, pulling on his socks. "I'm sure the phone lines between Washington and Moscow and Beijing will be burning up, but that's just words. As soon as the deal's done, it's too late, and that's what seems to happen far too often in today's world. We talk and talk and talk as if we're negotiating with reasonable people, but we're not. We're negotiating with dictators. They don't care. They'll say all the right things, shake hands, smile for the cameras, but in the end, they still do what they want. And then we in the West always act surprised as if we couldn't believe they had been lying the entire time and went ahead and did the unthinkable. Remember, we're talking about two countries here who coordinated the invasion of Ukraine so that it didn't interfere with the Winter Olympics in Beijing. It was a terrible strategic decision on Moscow's part, and probably cost them the war, but they couldn't risk pissing off the Chinese and the Chinese didn't give a shit whether hundreds of thousands of Ukrainians died. All they cared about was it might tarnish all the good PR they were getting from the Olympics."

"If talk doesn't cut it, what does? It's not like we can go to war with these countries."

"No, we certainly can't. But force is the only thing these people understand, and I have a feeling we're going to have to get our hands particularly dirty if we have any hope of stopping this." He pulled his pants up then stood, buttoning them then zipping his fly. She handed him his shirt and he took it. "Where is he?"

"He's in his room."

"Cameras?"

"One, though Larry did indicate there was a beating room in the basement."

Kane chuckled. "Move him into it. It's time Victor and I got acquainted."

Operations Center 3, CIA Headquarters

Langley, Virginia

Child spun in his chair, staring at the ceiling, Sherrie's comms playing overhead. "I don't know about you, but if she was my girlfriend, I wouldn't want him alone with her, naked or clothed."

Packman agreed. "I wouldn't want my boyfriend alone with him, and I know Kane's straight."

The doors hissed open and Leroux entered. "Report."

Tong, who had ignored the conversation, responded. "Kane's just told Sherrie to move Victor into the basement for an off-camera interview."

"Good. It's about damn time we get some answers."

Child's eyebrows shot up. "So, we're going to let him beat this guy? Doesn't that violate some laws?"

Leroux sat at his station, logging in. "I have a funny feeling that Kane will be intimidating enough or persuasive enough for Victor to give us what he knows before it comes to that, but the president has authorized any and all means to get the proof he needs."

"What's he going to do with it?" asked Tong.

"Obviously, every diplomatic means will be used to try to put a stop to it, but the White House doubts that'll work. All they need is the initial transfer to happen and it's too late."

Child leaned forward. "What does that mean, if they already know diplomacy's going to fail?" His voice trailed off as his stomach churned. He hadn't been working here for long, but he had been exposed to things he could never have imagined were actually occurring in the world, things the average American had no clue about, though he couldn't imagine anything more serious than this.

Leroux looked at him, his face grim. "The Pentagon is preparing military options for the president to consider."

"Holy shit!"

God help us all.

CIA Safe House
Moscow, Russia

"Where the hell is it?"

Kane tightened his grip on Victor's throat, the young man's face turning a darker shade of red as he desperately struggled to loosen the iron grip.

"Listen, Victor, you're the one who contacted us, not the other way around, but I didn't come all this way for nothing. Now, where the hell is the intel?" He loosened his grip slightly and Victor gasped for breath, the healthy pale of a man trapped in a winter climate for months returning rapidly.

"I can't do it. They'll kill me."

Kane wasn't surprised by the cold feet. It wasn't unusual in this business, but some things were too important to allow second thoughts to get in the way. "Listen, I know you want to do the right thing, that's why you contacted us, and now we're here. You're only in danger if they find out. Give me the intel, and I can get you out."

Victor stared at him, fear in his eyes. "And my family?"

Kane eyeballed him. "You're not married, and you don't have any children. What family are you talking about?"

"My parents, my sisters."

"There's no way in hell your parents would agree to extraction. And your sisters are barely teenagers. We'd never extract kids without their parents."

Victor sniffed hard. "Then I'm not telling you anything."

Kane had read the man's file. Normally, he would be considered a nobody in the grand scheme of things, a relatively recent hire in the Russian president's office. The fact he was fluent in six languages and a bit of a prodigy, combined with his wealthy family's long-time standing within the president's party, had him snapped up the moment he graduated from university.

His position meant access to information someone so junior would rarely be privy to. Even though he might be exposed to classified information, the Russians would still be careful, as any government would. People that age tended to be idealistic, lacking an understanding of how the world actually worked, believing it was their moral obligation to reveal things they didn't agree with, without thinking through the consequences of their actions.

But the kid's hesitation had him now doubting whether his claims were legit. Had he just heard something? Had he lied about having proof? Could he just be a spoiled brat dodging the draft?

"I think you're full of shit."

Victor's eyes shot wide. "No, I'm telling the truth."

"I don't think you have the intel. I think you're just yanking our chain so you can dodge the draft."

Victor vehemently shook his head. "No, I'm telling you the truth, but the files are the only bargaining chip I have."

"Your claim is too outrageous. Without proof, it's just the wild claims of some kid."

"I'm not a kid. I'm telling the truth."

"Why would your country do this? You have to realize how dangerous this is, how out of control things could become?"

Victor threw his hands up in the air, anger flaring in his eyes. "You Americans are unbelievable! You slap illegal sanctions on my country for defending ourselves against fascists in Ukraine, you cripple our economy, supply weapons to our enemies resulting in the death of our soldiers, and you wonder why we would do such a thing? We're desperate! People are suffering! The world is against us because of your lies! So when my president figures out a way out of this mess, a way to guarantee our future..." He shook his head. "No, I've made a mistake. I can't do this. I have to go."

Kane ignored the change of mind. "Listen, kid, I realize you admire your president. Far too many Russians do, but you know this is wrong, and you have to know war is wrong. If this deal goes through, yes, your country will have money and be able to avoid the pain of the sanctions, but it also means it will be able to wage war for years to come. And if they win in Ukraine, what's next? Moldova? Georgia? The Baltics?

Western Europe? And if you go to war with NATO, you will lose. You'll either lose the war, or it will go nuclear, and we'll all lose. We don't have a choice here, and I do mean we. Together, we can try to stop this, but I need that proof. I need something to show my people so we can take action and stop the biggest threat to world peace since the Cuban Missile Crisis. Please, kid, give me a way to save your country from the biggest mistake it has ever made."

Victor stared at him, tears in his eyes. "I can't. I can't betray my country. I'm sorry, I was wrong to have contacted you."

Kane delivered a gut punch, retightening his grip. "Unfortunately, you don't have a say in the matter anymore. The more you talk, the more I'm convinced this intel is real. Just hand it over and this all ends. Nobody will ever know we got the info from you. But if it's true, withholding it could prolong and potentially expand the hostilities. Thousands, if not millions of lives are at stake. Or is this intel bullshit, just an excuse to get out, to get to America before you're drafted?"

Victor's eyes bulged at the idea. "No, I swear I'm no coward. If my country wants me to fight, then I'll fight."

"Then why did you contact us?"

Victor's shoulders slumped. "Because this is too much. It's too serious. It can't be allowed to happen."

Kane let go of Victor's neck and took a step back. "If you feel that way, then you have to tell me. You know it's the right thing to do."

Victor's chin sagged into his chest as tears rolled down his cheeks. "I'm terrified."

"Good. Then you know you're doing the right thing, that it's important, and because of that, I'll get you out, but I can't get that ball rolling until you give me that intel."

Victor slowly nodded. He reached down and took off his left shoe, lifted the liner, and retrieved a small memory card. He handed it to Kane then put his shoe back on.

"This is it?"

"Yes. It's a translation of a document, a response from the Chinese government to a proposal from the Kremlin. I was never supposed to see it, but the senior translator was sick and the president's office urgently needed the document translated, so I was tasked."

Kane held up the tiny memory storage device. "What am I going to find on here?"

"The Chinese response to a Russian proposal to transfer the bulk of our nuclear arsenal to Chinese management."

Kane's eyes narrowed. "Management?"

"It's not a sale. It's a lease. They take the weapons and maintain them, and in exchange, they pay my government a leasing fee starting at ten billion Euros per year and going up from there, for the next thirty years. And they guarantee their support militarily and economically against any and all of our enemies." Victor sighed. "My country is securing its future by selling its past."

Kane grunted. "A past it can no longer afford. Of course, peace would never occur to your president. NATO would be more than happy to pay for the decommissioning of all the weapons and lower our own stockpiles to match. Instead, your dictator is ensuring that the world remains on the brink of nuclear war."

"Now you see why I'm doing what I'm doing. This can't be allowed to happen. It's too dangerous. At least we have a seventy-year history of never having used the weapons. I don't trust the Chinese not to. And I don't trust the Chinese to keep their word should NATO decide to invade when they discover what we've given up."

"NATO would never invade first."

"Yeah, right. You expect me to believe a CIA agent?"

"Believe what you want, it doesn't matter. You've done the right thing. Now we need to get you safely out of here and get this intel into the right hands to see what we can do to stop it before it's too late."

Presidential Executive Office, The Kremlin

Moscow, Russia

Peskov stared at himself in the mirror, frowning at the dark purple bruise on his throat. It could have been worse. He could be dead like the others, but whoever it was that had violated the sanctity of his home hadn't killed anyone who wasn't armed. The Chinese had been contacted about the incident and were gravely concerned about the security breach, and the president was already worried the Chinese might scrap the deal.

Beijing had insisted the leak hadn't come from their end and that Zhang wasn't even aware of what was going on. Peskov had just finished a video call with the real Zhang, and while he appeared identical to the man who had assaulted him yesterday, the voice was dramatically different. He assured him he was still in Beijing and even carried his camera around his private home, holding it out the window to see the streets below. The Chinese were convinced the leak was from the Russian end, and insisted it be plugged before the deal proceeded.

And that job now fell on him, a potentially impossible task. The good thing about his job was that in Russia, leaks could be plugged by scapegoats, not necessarily guilty parties. The question was, who could he plausibly pin it on? This was one of his country's most highly classified documents. If the breach were too ridiculous, too far from the inner office, it would suggest to the Chinese that their security was woefully inadequate and that Russia couldn't be trusted to keep things a secret.

This was a thirty-year deal, a massive transfer of material wealth, a nation's legacy to another nation in exchange for a monetary lifeline and a mutual defense pact that nobody seriously believed the Chinese would honor. But as long as the money kept coming in, that was all that was truly critical. Despite the bluster on the state-controlled media, everybody knew NATO would never attack first. Russia's borders were safe. It didn't need its nuclear arsenal. Those days were gone.

What it needed was money, stable payments that would allow them to rebuild, diversify their economy, and undo the harm Western sanctions had inflicted. With this deal and the conventional weapons deal, they should win the war within a year, then decide what to do next. Lessons had been learned, costly lessons, and they would be better prepared should the president continue his plan to bring all ethnic Russians under his umbrella, no matter how small the population. And once they started winning, the public would be on their side as victory after victory played out on the television screens.

The young men of Russia would clamor to join the fight, and those that had fled like cowards would return once the punishment of their families began. It was a bright future, a future he looked forward to seeing and guiding, but it would only happen if he could plug the leak to the satisfaction of the Chinese.

He stared at the list he had written of everyone who had access to the document. It was short. Six names, including his and the president's. There was only one name on the list that he could possibly point the finger at, and that was young Victor Stepanov, who was never supposed to have seen the document. Unfortunately for him, there was a plausible reason for why he had, a reason that would make the office look bad in the eyes of the Chinese, though could be perceived as forgivable. It was a one-time lapse due to a confluence of circumstances—a birthday party that had gone far too late and far too hard, a young man in a position merely because of who his father was, though dedicated enough to show up the next day, unlike his colleagues. He was the only resource available capable of translating a document, a resource they had assumed they could trust due to whom his father was.

He hated to do it, yet he had no choice. He was still convinced the leak must have come from Firouz, but the Chinese had sworn up and down they had inspected the envelope and were certain it had never been opened before they received it. There was no point in arguing with them. They were in control. Russia needed China far more than China needed Russia, so if the Chinese insisted the leak came from the

Russian end, then it came from the Russian end, and poor Victor would pay the price regardless of his innocence.

He picked up his phone and his secretary answered. "Yes, sir?"

"Get me Nikitin."

CIA Safe House
Moscow, Russia

Victor sat in his room, staring at the television screen, watching the news reports that he no longer believed, racked with guilt over what he was doing. The more he thought about it, the more he wondered whether what he was doing was right. Certainly, in the eyes of the law it wasn't, but that didn't matter. Was it morally wrong? He had always felt nuclear weapons were a necessary evil. And who was he to say the arrangement being made wasn't what was best for his country? If the Western news reports he had been reading over the past couple of days were accurate, his country was at best not losing the war, but they certainly weren't winning it.

Hundreds of thousands might be dead on his side alone. Countless women and children on the other side had also perished. Cities and towns lay in ruin and a nuclear power plant was on the brink of a catastrophic meltdown. His country was the aggressor. His country was in the wrong, yet no one seemed interested in peace, the Ukrainian leadership now insisting that every Russian soldier be ejected from their country, including Crimea, an area traditionally Russian and had been gifted to Ukraine in 1954 to celebrate the 300th anniversary of the Treaty of Pereyaslav. It was populated mostly by Russians, with far less than 20% of the population ethnic Ukrainians, and had returned to Russian control in 2014. Surely, they should be allowed to keep that. God knows the price paid was too heavy to walk away with nothing.

Had people not learned from history, from World War I? When you humiliated your defeated opponent, once it finished licking its wounds, like any abused animal, it finally reaches its breaking point and attacks. The result of the Treaty of Versailles was Nazi Germany and a world war far worse than the first. This time, the allies had rebuilt Germany, rebuilt Japan, and they were now stable, thriving democracies with two of the largest economies in the world.

Russia had obviously made a mistake. Should it be destroyed, humiliated, crippled for a generation? That seemed to be what the West wanted. Perhaps what the president was doing was the only way out of this mess. Save the economy, save the country for another generation, win the war, then put this unfortunate mess behind them.

A breaking news alert appeared on the screen and his eyes shot wide as his father's name appeared in white letters on a bright red background, cameras flashing as his parents and two sisters were led out of their home in handcuffs and put in the back of separate police cars. He turned up the volume as Chief of Staff Peskov appeared on the screen.

"Alexei Stepanov has been taken into custody pending charges of treason. His family has been taken into protective custody while we search for his son, Victor Stepanov." His photo appeared on the screen and he nearly vomited. "It's believed that Mr. Stepanov's son collaborated with him to steal official state secrets by taking advantage of his new position as a translator within the president's office. We are asking for the public's assistance in locating Victor Stepanov so we can confirm the extent of his family's involvement in what he's done."

Peskov stared into the camera as if peering directly into Victor's eyes. "Victor, I urge you, turn yourself in. I have no doubt you didn't realize what you were doing and someone coerced you into this, but until we know your side of things, we're forced to assume your father is the reason you did what you did." Peskov walked away from the bank of microphones and the news report resumed, the anchor summarizing the story so far.

Victor turned off the television and stared at his hands, clasped in front of him.

What am I going to do?

"You're going to want to see this."

Kane looked up from the kitchen table at Jane, standing in the doorway. "What?" he asked as he rose along with Sherrie.

"News report. Looks like your kid's family was just arrested and he's a wanted man. They're saying he colluded with his father to steal state secrets."

126

Kane cursed as he took a seat in front of the television, continuing to chow down on his BLT sandwich. He swallowed a bite. "He's got a TV in his room, doesn't he?"

"Yes."

Kane sighed and turned to Sherrie. "You better go check on him."

The alarm panel chirped and Larry cursed. "Front door!" He bolted toward the main entrance to the house as Kane casually took another bite of his sandwich. Sherrie stared at him incredulously.

"Aren't you concerned?"

Kane shrugged as he chewed, holding his hand up to provide a polite screen as he broke every mother's cardinal rule.

Don't talk with your mouth full.

"We got the intel. If he doesn't want to give us the opportunity to honor our end of the deal, that's his choice. He's not a prisoner."

"But he's going to get himself killed."

"That's possible." Kane swallowed and activated his comms. "Control, Wild One, we've got a runner. Can you pick him up on satellite, over?"

"Stand by, Wild One," Leroux replied a moment later. "We've got him heading north of your location. He's about to get on a city bus."

"There's some debate on this end on whether we should go fetch him."

"We have the intel. Is there anything else he could possibly tell us?"

"I doubt it. That one document is the only thing he was ever exposed to. However, if he does get himself captured or turns himself in, the Russians are going to know that we know what's going on, and that we were behind what happened at Peskov's house."

"True," agreed Leroux. "I guess the question is, do we care if the Russians know we know? Is that a bad thing? Our president's about to hit them with that piece of info any time now."

Kane sighed. "I'd hate to see the kid get hurt for doing the right thing, but we can't exactly be chasing him around the city and exposing our operation."

"I'll run it by the Chief and see what he thinks."

"Sounds good. Keep tracking him and let me know what the brass decides. Wild One, out."

Larry returned with Jane, out of breath. "Little shit got on a bus. He's in the wind."

Kane tapped his ear. "Control is tracking him. Waiting on word on whether we're supposed to care."

Sherrie fetched her sandwich from the kitchen and joined him in front of the TV. "I still don't see why you're not concerned. He should at least be protected from himself."

"Not our job. One thing you need to learn about this business is that we're not guidance counselors. We're Worf, not Troi."

"Speak for yourself, I prefer to think of myself as Tasha."

Kane growled suggestively at her. "Good choice. But like I was saying, our job is to protect our country. He had information we needed. We got that information and we were prepared to fulfill the bargain we made to get it. Nothing said he had to take us up on the offer. He can change his mind at any time. People change their mind all the time, have second thoughts. If we haven't got what we needed out of them before they change their mind, then sometimes we go after them and make them reconsider. But we can't be risking our lives and our network because a twenty-two-year-old kid saw his family in handcuffs on TV and wants to save them. And who knows, maybe he's doing the right thing. The Russians know his family has nothing to do with this. He turns himself in, gets his parents and sisters set free, then he's the only one paying the price."

Sherrie frowned, pushing away her sandwich, her appetite apparently lost. "I still think it's kind of cold."

"It's not called a Cold War for nothing. And trust me, we're knee-deep in version 2.0 of it." He jerked his chin toward the half-eaten sandwich. "You going to finish that?"

She eyed it with disdain. "No, I don't have the stomach for it anymore."

Kane grabbed it. "Good. I'm still starving." He took a bite and his eyes widened. "Why is it that someone else's food always tastes better, even when it's the same damn thing?"

"It must be my lip gloss."

Kane leaned over and gave her a peck on the lips then licked his own. "Nah, that's not it."

Sherrie gave him a look. "I'm telling Chris you did that."

Kane grinned. "He would've wanted to know the answer too."

North of the CIA Safe House
Moscow, Russia

Victor stared out the window of the bus as it pulled away, the American chasing him giving up as the nearly empty vehicle gained speed.

"Please pay your fare, sir."

Victor flinched and turned to the driver, wide-eyed. "What?"

"You have to pay your fare or get off."

Victor slapped at his pockets, realizing they were empty, the Americans having confiscated everything including his wallet and phone. "I don't have any money."

"Then you're going to have to get off." The driver applied the brakes, slowing them, and Victor panicked.

"No, wait! You don't understand! The Americans are chasing me!"

"Yeah, sure they are, kid."

"No, I'm Victor Stepanov, the one they're looking for from the news. I want to turn myself in, but if you stop the bus, the Americans will get me."

"Oh my God, it is him!" cried a woman seated farther back, holding up her cellphone for the others to see, his photo from the news glowing on the display.

Victor pointed to the American still visible in the distance. "That's one of them!"

Everyone turned. "Oh no! There *is* someone there!" exclaimed an elderly gentleman.

"Go, go, go!" pleaded another, and the driver lifted his foot off the brake and hammered on the gas, the beast barely reacting, though the deceleration ended.

"You said you wanted to turn yourself in?"

"Yes, sir."

The driver pointed at the nearest seat. "Then sit."

Victor complied and the driver got on his radio, calling for help. Victor's pulse pounded in his ears as he struggled to catch his breath, his mind muddled with conflicting thoughts, terrified at what was to come. They would beat and torture him mercilessly, of that, he had no doubt. This was, after all, Russia. The question was, would it be worth it? Could he save his family from his crime?

If he were completely truthful up front, would they be merciful? Would they even beat him at all? He was quite certain he would be executed, and while the thought tortured his soul, knowing his family would go on living provided him with some small comfort. Yet would

131

it go on? They might be alive, but his father would never be trusted again. He would be shunned by his peers, by the party, by the president, and no doubt would have all of his assets confiscated by the state, as had happened to other men in his position who had somehow failed their leader. To go from having billions to enjoy life without a want or need in the world going unmet, to potentially begging on the street was unthinkable, and in his mind, possibly worse than death.

Even if he turned himself in, he might not be saving them.

Had he made a mistake? He stared out the window, a large billboard urging people to join the military and the fight. He had done what he had to save his country, and now he was trying to save his family. Which took priority? Which was more important, family or country? Four people or 146 million people?

He squeezed his eyes shut, temporarily stemming the tears threatening to flow. The question was irrelevant. He had already done his part. There was nothing more he could give the Americans. They had the intel, and it was the only piece of information he had been exposed to. He knew nothing more. His job was done. It was up to the Americans now to stop what was going on and save his country from itself. Now, all that mattered was his family. All he could do was pray that when he turned himself in, the authorities would be satisfied with that, and set his family free. He had no bargaining chips, nothing.

His eyes shot wide with an idea. There was no way anyone could prove he had handed over the intel. Could he leverage that to gain his family's freedom, set them free, put them on a flight to the West?

Set them free, otherwise, I tell the Americans what I know.

Could that work? And if it could, for how long? Once the Americans confronted his country with what they knew, his bluff would be found out. He assumed the Americans would act quickly on this. Time was of the essence. He likely had hours, not days, and if he were to hand himself over, how much time would be wasted before anyone would listen for him to make his demands? Would they even believe he had made an arrangement with someone, that should something happen to him the information would be released?

He had to get off the bus.

He shot to his feet and stepped toward the front. "Stop the bus."

"What?" The driver glanced at him, bewildered. "Those aren't my instructions."

Victor desperately sought a solution then pointed behind them. "We just passed a police car. Stop the bus. I want to hand myself over to them directly."

The driver refused. "No, those aren't my instructions."

Victor cursed, panic overwhelming him. He had to get off the bus. He had made the wrong decision. This wasn't going to save his family, and that was all he wanted now. "Sorry." He reached out and grabbed the steering wheel, yanking it toward him. The bus careened to the right, the driver cursing in shock as he applied the brakes, causing them to tilt then tip onto the left-side wheels. They crashed into a storefront window, bringing them to a jarring halt, the bus teetering for a moment before coming down to rest on all its wheels. The few passengers were in a panic, screaming, crying, and the bus driver on instinct reached out and opened the doors.

"I'm so sorry!" cried Victor as he bolted, kicking his way through the debris and emerging onto the sidewalk. He ducked down an alleyway then ran with no idea on how to enact his plan that might be the only hope of saving his family.

Operations Center 3, CIA Headquarters
Langley, Virginia

"There he goes," said Child, pointing at the display. Leroux watched as a figure wearing clothing that matched Victor's sprinted from the scene of the accident that he was certain was intentional.

"I have a funny feeling young Victor has changed his mind," said Packman.

Leroux had little doubt Victor had indeed changed his mind, but to what end? Nothing had changed. Those sober second thoughts brought on by being given enough time to think things through, often made one realize how stupid a rash decision actually was. But did he want to come in, or had he come up with his own plan to save his family? He turned to Tong. "Let Kane know where he is. Send a vehicle to pick him up."

"And if he doesn't want to go?"

Leroux frowned as he thought for a moment. "Then let him go. But make sure it's clear to him that this is his last chance."

"Is there anything we can do to help his family?" asked Packman.

"No, we can't stage a rescue. They're of no importance beyond humanitarian, and even then, not a lot of people would have any sympathy for them considering Alexei Stepanov's staunch support of the Russian president in the war. No, Victor's family is on their own, but we still have a commitment we made with Victor that we have to keep if, and I stress *if*, he still wants to take us up on our offer of asylum."

Tong fit her headset in place. "I'll let Kane know."

Leroux watched as Victor emerged onto a street in a shopping district, pedestrian traffic light as the shops were closed. "Tell him he better hurry up. Otherwise, this guy's going to get himself arrested sooner rather than later."

Presidential Executive Office, The Kremlin
Moscow, Russia

Peskov cursed at the report he had just received. Victor had been on a bus asking to turn himself in, then had apparently changed his mind, causing a crash and escaping before the unit sent to bring him in could reach him. "Shut down the entire area. Nothing gets in or out without being searched. Go house to house if you have to. I want him found."

"Yes, sir."

He slammed the receiver down in the cradle, the satisfying abuse of the innocent device something you couldn't get away with when using a cellphone. They would find him, but it could take time, time they didn't have. Everything was on hold until this leak was plugged. Everything on the Russian end was still moving forward under the assumption the deal would eventually go through. Missile systems were being prepared across the nation for the rapid transfer into Chinese hands. It was the Chinese that were refusing to accept them at the moment.

If this deal didn't go through, someone would pay, and it would go far beyond the Stepanov family. Someone with power, with clout, with responsibility would ultimately be hanged should the deal fall through. And with so few people in the know, there was a very good chance he could be the one taking the blame. This was bullshit. He had put together the deal. Yes, it was an idea poached from a brainstorming session, but he had constructed the agreement and the president had put his signature on it. The man would no doubt take full credit should things work out, and that was fine. That's the way things were in Russia and the world over. The leader took credit. The difference between Russia and America was that the leader rarely took blame, and there was no ballot box to answer to. Well, there was no ballot box to answer to that couldn't be stuffed.

He stared at a photo of his family taken two years ago while vacationing in the Crimea, the Black Sea resort even more stunning with Russian flags flying overhead rather than Ukrainian. Blue skies over golden wheat fields. Ridiculous. If he were made the scapegoat, his family would suffer horribly and his children would have no future. He had to bring Victor in, but if he couldn't, he needed to frame someone else. The question was who?

His phone beeped and he hit the intercom. "Yes?"

"Sir, you're not going to believe this, but I've got Victor Stepanov on the line for you."

North of the CIA Safe House

Moscow, Russia

Victor pressed the borrowed phone to his ear, the girl he had charmed with a story of being mugged, standing nearby with her two friends giggling over how cute he was. He turned away, shielding them from the conversation. "Hello, sir, it's Victor Stepanov."

"Victor. You know you're in a spot of trouble, don't you?"

"Yes, sir. That's why I'm calling. I want to do the right thing."

"Then turn yourself in."

"I'm willing to do that, sir. But on one condition."

There was a pause, and any hint of false friendliness in Peskov's tone was gone. "What's that?"

"I want my family set free and put on a plane to America. Once they land, I'll turn myself in."

"Unacceptable!"

Victor almost lost control of his bladder as a wave of weakness swept through him.

"You'll hand yourself over immediately, and depending on what you tell us, should we believe your family is innocent, then we'll let them go."

Victor squeezed his eyes shut, pinching the bridge of his nose. "Sir, with all due respect, you know my family is innocent. The lies that are being told on television are just that, lies. They were told in order to get me to turn myself in, and they worked. I'm willing to do that, but not before my parents and my sisters are safe."

"If they're innocent like you say, and yes, we know they're innocent, then they have nothing to worry about."

"Sir, you and I both know with what I did, my father's position is forever compromised. I've seen what happens to people who cross the president. He's finished. Everything will be taken from him and he still might end up in prison. I'm not asking that they be allowed to keep their wealth. All I'm asking is that they be allowed to keep their lives and start over somewhere else where they won't be persecuted for my actions."

There was a pause. "What actions?"

Victor gulped. If he didn't know better, he had just detected a hint of surprise in Peskov's voice. Did they not know? Was this all a bluff from their end? He had just assumed when he saw the broadcast that they had figured out what he had done. But perhaps they hadn't. Perhaps something more was going on here and he was being set up as the scapegoat, and it was mere coincidence that he was guilty. But it was too late now. He had just admitted he had done something wrong, but it could mean he might have some leverage here, for they wouldn't have had time to think about this scenario.

"I copied the response from China that I was tasked to translate then I made contact with the Americans, offering it to them in exchange for asylum."

The string of curses that erupted from Peskov's end of the phone confirmed this was an entirely unexpected revelation. "Why would you do such a thing?"

"Because what the president is doing is wrong."

"Who are you to decide that?"

"I'm a citizen of this country, but I think my motivations are irrelevant at this point. There's no turning back now."

"So, you've already given the information to the Americans?"

"No."

Another pause. "You said you made contact with them."

"I did, but I refused to give them the information until I was safely out of the country."

"Then why are you calling me now?"

"Because I decided my family is more important. If you set them free and put them on a plane for America, I will turn myself in and the Americans will never know about the agreement between us and China."

A siren sounded in the distance causing his heart to leap into his throat. He had forgotten they could be tracing him. "I'll leave you to consider my proposal and I'll call you back in about an hour. Don't bother tracing this call. I borrowed a phone from a stranger on the street and she doesn't deserve to be harassed over what I've done." He ended the call before Peskov could say anything else then turned back to the girls with a smile. He handed the phone over. "Thank you so much."

The girl stared at her feet then up at him. "Can I get your number?"

He smiled. "Not much point. You'd only be calling whoever stole it."

Her cheeks flushed. "I suppose you're right."

One of her friends elbowed her. "Write your number down."

Purses were searched for a pen and a scrap piece of paper, and moments later he was walking away with the gorgeous girl's phone number that he would get rid of as soon as he was out of sight, because if he were picked up by the authorities, her life would be over too.

A car pulled up beside him and he paid it no mind.

"Hey, kid, get in."

He spun to see the American who had interrogated him leaning out the driver's side window.

And this time he did lose control of his bladder.

Kane frowned as Victor hurried away. He lifted his foot off the brake and the car rolled forward. "Listen, kid, I just want to talk. After we talk, you can leave. You're not our prisoner. We already got what we want from you, and all we want to do is fulfill our end of the bargain. But if you decide you don't want our help, then you're free to walk."

Sirens grew louder and Victor stopped.

"Listen, I don't know if those are for you, but they could be. This entire area is being locked down. Get in and we'll talk. Nothing more."

Victor sighed then rounded the front bumper, climbing in the passenger seat. Kane pulled away from the curb and back onto the proper side of the road, a couple of horns honking in protest. He gave them a friendly wave then caught the distinct odor of urine. Victor had his hands clasped over his nether regions, shame on his face.

"Listen, kid, it's nothing to feel bad about. I've met Spetsnaz guys who pissed their pants. Fear isn't something to be ashamed of. It's something you learn to harness. You just haven't had a chance to learn how yet, and hopefully you never need to."

"Did you ever piss your pants?"

Kane laughed. "Only when drunk, but I've come damn close many times, let me tell you. In my line of work, you control the fear, harness the alertness it gives you, and then push through the situation. Now, let's talk about what's going on. Just so you know, our agreement still stands. We're willing to get you out of the country and back to the United States exactly as we promised. Are you still interested in that?"

Victor sighed, staring out the window. "All I care about is my family."

"You do realize that if you hand yourself over, they're going to torture you and then probably execute you."

"I…" Victor's voice cracked. "I know, but I don't have a choice. They're my family." The tears flowed. "They're my baby sisters." He turned to Kane, his eyes red. "Can you help them?"

"I'd be lying to you if I said I could. There's no way we can get them out, even if we were willing to."

"Would you give them asylum?"

Kane regarded him. "I suppose it's possible, but you can only grant asylum to someone who isn't in prison."

"I'm working on a deal."

Kane glanced over at the kid. "Wait a minute. What kind of deal?"

"I called Dimitri Peskov. He's the Russian—"

"I know who he is. When did you call him?"

"Just before you pulled up."

"And what was said?"

"Well, it's kind of weird, but I don't think he had any idea I had actually stolen the document. He seemed surprised."

Kane processed this new piece of information, and it made sense. The way the intel had been stolen was essentially undetectable, and until Washington acted on it, the Russians wouldn't know it had been taken. What was likely going on was that they were reacting to his infiltration of Peskov's home because he had impersonated a Chinese official. Beijing was probably contacted to confirm the real Zhang's location, and were forced to admit what was going on, which could be putting the entire agreement in jeopardy. A scapegoat was needed. Victor was low man on the totem pole and was in the chain of custody of the document. The Russians in their zeal to blame someone had accidentally named the correct person. "That makes sense."

"It does?"

"There's a lot more going on than you realize. Chances are, they're just looking for somebody to blame on their end. You're the least important name in the structure they could come up with, and they just got lucky."

"And my family pays the price."

"You said you were working on a deal. What is it?"

"I told them that I hadn't handed over the intel yet, that I said I would only do it once I was safely in the United States."

Kane's head bobbed, impressed the kid had come up with the idea on his own. "So, you told them that if they set your family free, you'll turn yourself in, and the intel will have never been handed over?"

"Yes, but that they had to be put on a plane to America, and once they were safely there, I'd turn myself in."

Kane scratched his chin then made a left turn. "It's a good plan and it might just work, but it takes too long."

"What do you mean?"

"A flight from Moscow to New York is about ten hours. All we need to do is get your parents into a NATO country. Warsaw is two hours away. Tell them to send your parents to Warsaw. My people will pick them up there and get them to the States."

"You'll do that?"

"I can't promise my government will agree because of who your father is, but I'm making a personal guarantee to you that if you can get your family to Warsaw, I will get them to America regardless of what my government agrees to."

"How?"

Kane chuckled. "I've been in this business for a while now and have a lot of contacts and a lot of people who owe me favors. Deal?"

Victor stared at him wide-eyed. "Deal."

"Now the question is, what do we do about you?"

Victor's shoulders slumped as the excitement of perhaps saving his parents gave way to the reality that it still meant his torture and death. "I don't see that I have many options."

"Well, first of all, we're going to get you back to the safe house so you can clean up and empty that bladder the right way. We're going to get you that memory card back so you actually have something to hand over, because they're never going to buy that you threw it away, and then we'll see if we can figure out some other way to get your ass out. But all this has to happen quick."

"Why is that?"

"Because as soon as our president goes public with what we know, they'll know you're lying and then all bets are off."

Presidential Executive Office, The Kremlin
Moscow, Russia

Peskov looked up as FSB Director Nikitin entered his office. "I wasn't expecting you so quickly."

"I was still in the building. I understand you've discovered something?"

Peskov pointed. "Close the door and have a seat."

Nikitin shut the door then sat, saying nothing. Peskov had always found the man incredibly intimidating, and was well aware the head of the FSB had the power to make him disappear with a snap of his fingers.

"I've identified the source of the leak."

Nikitin cocked an eyebrow. "You have?"

"Yes, it's Victor Stepanov."

"Interesting. Is this a theory?"

"No, I just got off the phone with him and he confessed. He copied the document then contacted the Americans to make a deal. They're to grant him asylum in exchange for the information."

"Interesting. Can you prove that?"

"You think I'm lying?"

"No, however, proof is always better than someone's word. If you truly want to demonstrate to the Chinese that you've solved the problem, a recorded confession would certainly do that, especially one offered voluntarily as opposed to under torture."

"Unfortunately or fortunately, depending on how one looks at it, things aren't recorded on my line."

"Not from your end."

Peskov's eyes narrowed. "What do you mean?"

"How did he call you?"

"He said from a cellphone he borrowed from some girl on the street."

"Then we can get the number and see if we have any intercepts on it."

"I suppose that's possible. I'll have it provided to you. What do you think the chances are that you have a recording?"

Nikitin shrugged. "Hard to say. We're not as good as the Americans yet, but we're getting better. We might get lucky, but let's assume we don't. He called you for what purpose?"

"He's claiming he hasn't handed the intel over to the Americans yet. He wants his parents on a plane to America. Once they're safely there, he'll turn himself in and give us back the intel."

"Interesting. And you believe he hasn't handed it over?"

Peskov sighed. "That's the question, isn't it? He's just a kid, twenty-two years old. It's pretty ballsy for him to call somebody in my position and try to bluff."

"It is, but I've seen younger men on the battlefield with balls that would impress anyone twice their age. Never assume less of someone simply because you have a bias against their age. If he hasn't handed over the intel, then why did they infiltrate your house?"

"I was thinking about that, and the timing doesn't work out, does it? The reply arrived two days ago. He remained at work for the rest of his shift. There's no way he could have contacted the Americans before leaving work and even then, what did he do? March right up to the embassy? I doubt it. Your people would've noticed, I'm sure."

"We would have."

"So, he made contact in some other manner. He wouldn't use a phone, because again, you'd have caught that, so he had to do it in person somehow. If he mailed them something, they might have received it today, but more likely they wouldn't have, so he had to do it in person. Even if he made contact two nights ago, there's no way he would have been taken seriously enough for the Americans to send an agent in within hours of that. These things do take time, don't they?"

Nikitin agreed. "They do, even for the almighty Americans. I agree with you, what happened at your home had nothing to do with Mr. Stepanov's betrayal."

"So then, the Americans already knew?"

"They already knew something was going on, that's for certain. The question is what do they know? I'm not privy to what's actually going on here. Apparently, even my security clearance isn't high enough."

Peskov splayed his hands in apology. "The president's orders, I'm sorry."

Nikitin dismissed the apology. "Secrets are my business, and I'm never surprised when someone wants to keep their own. You said you were surprised the Chinese would send someone to discuss things in person, and now we know why the Americans did it."

"Why is that?"

"Because they didn't know about the reply. I think you're right. I think their information is coming from the arms dealer's end of things."

"Do you think he was the leak?"

"Possibly, but more likely, the Americans were watching him and saw him with you and recorded your conversation, to which you already admitted he referenced the envelope. That would've piqued their interest, and we know they're highly concerned with the potential of China selling us weapons, since it could change the course of the war."

"You think they would risk sending someone in like they did?"

Nikitin regarded him. "Well, they did, so obviously I would."

Peskov bristled at Nikitin's implication that the question was stupid. "I meant sending someone in over a simple arms deal rather than what's actually going on."

Nikitin sighed. "This grows increasingly frustrating. I highly recommend you ask the president that I be read in on this file. The Americans already know something's going on and they might know exactly what's going on if young Victor is lying about having not handed over the intel already. If you want me to be effective, I need to know what's going on. It doesn't need to go beyond me. No one else in the FSB will be aware, but it'll allow me to direct resources properly and to better assess where the risks lie so we can contain the spread."

Peskov pursed his lips as he considered Nikitin's request. The man was right, they needed the resources of the FSB applied correctly, not blindly, if they had any hope of dealing with this problem. He tapped the intercom and his secretary answered.

"Yes, sir?"

"Find out if the president is in his office."

"Right away, sir."

He disconnected the intercom then turned to Nikitin. "Be careful what you wish for. Somebody's going down for this and you might not want to be on such a short list."

CIA Safe House
Moscow, Russia

Kane entered the safe house and was greeted by Larry and Jane then Sherrie as she rushed down the stairs. She gave him a hug.

"Thank God. Langley says this entire area is crawling with police."

"Yeah, we won't be able to move much pretty soon. Our friend here phoned Dimitri Peskov with a pretty ballsy bluff."

Sherrie reached out and squeezed Victor's arm. "Are you all right?"

Victor shrugged. "I guess so."

Kane turned to Larry. "You've transmitted that intel, right?"

"Yeah. As soon as you gave me the chip."

"Good, then we don't need it?"

"Technically, no."

"Okay, go get it. I promised the kid he can have it back."

Jane's eyebrows shot up. "Oh?"

"He's trying to swing a deal. He'll hand himself and the chip over in exchange for his family being released and put on a plane to the States."

"And they've agreed to that?"

Victor shook his head. "No, but I'm supposed to call him"—he checked his watch—"in the next half-hour."

Kane continued. "I've suggested a tweak to his request. I'm suggesting his family be put on a plane to Warsaw and we can have people there pick them up. It narrows the timeframe dramatically."

Sherrie folded her arms, regarding Victor. "Well, we definitely want to narrow the window. There's no way the president's going to wait long enough for a flight from Moscow to the States. But even then, do you really think he'll wait? Victor's father isn't exactly in our good books."

Kane agreed. "No, I don't think he's going to wait at all, which is why we need to act fast. And this assumes the Russians are even interested in making a deal. If they aren't, then this is all moot regardless. But if they are, we need his family in the air and back on the ground as quickly as possible before that hotline between Washington and Moscow rings." He motioned to the stairs. "Victor, why don't you go take care of business. Larry, you get him that memory chip. I'm going to talk to Langley, see what we can swing."

Victor scurried up the stairs and Sherrie cocked an eyebrow. "What's his hurry?"

Kane lowered his voice. "The poor kid pissed himself."

Sherrie squinted, her eyes glistening, and she took Kane's hand, giving it a squeeze. "And here I thought you didn't care."

Operations Center 3, CIA Headquarters

Langley, Virginia

Leroux stared at the satellite footage from three days ago showing two of the intimidating RS-24 Yars missile systems rolling through the front doors of one of the hardened storage facilities, confirming not only what Kane had discovered earlier, but that at least two of the buildings contained these terrifying weapons. "Well, that's two, and Kane counted six, so we have at least eight here, probably more. Let's keep going back, see if we can find any more being brought in." He turned to Tong as a thought occurred to him. "Take a look at the photos that Kane took, see if we can determine what type of container is being used. We know that anything dealing with the missile systems will be highly classified, but they might have screwed up with the containers. There's no way they had them just sitting there waiting for this. They would've been specifically requested. If we can identify the container type, we can analyze our intercepts and see how many of them were requested, and where they were deployed to."

"I'm on it," replied Tong.

The speakers chirped overhead. "Control, Wild One, come in, over."

Leroux fit his headset in place and activated his comms. "Wild One, Control Actual. Go ahead."

"I've got the kid. He's back at the safe house, but we've got a situation."

Leroux tensed, well aware that security was pouring into the area after the incident on the bus. "What's that?"

"Victor called Peskov, told him that he hadn't handed the intel over yet and was willing to return it and hand himself over in exchange for his family being released and put on a plane stateside."

Leroux whistled. "That's quite the bluff."

"No shit. I need you to talk to the Chief. Victor's going to be calling Peskov back within thirty minutes. I've told him to change the destination to Warsaw. That'll limit flight time. I need to know, are we willing to pick his family up and get them into the underground railroad, and whether the president's willing to hold off long enough for us to make this happen."

Leroux frowned. "I doubt it. Alexei Stepanov has been a pain in our collective ass for years. I doubt they're willing to do him any favors."

"Well, perhaps someone should remind him that the wife and the two daughters are innocent. However, if we can't get the president to agree, let's at least see if we can find out when he plans to confront the Russians with what we know. At least then we'll know if this is even possible."

"Understood. I'll go talk to the Chief now and see what he says."

"Just in case Washington says no to this, can you tell me where Jack is?"

Leroux's eyebrows shot up. "Why?"

"Personal."

"He's in Austria visiting a mutual friend before he returns to duty."

"Copy that. Let me know what the White House says. Remember, thirty minutes. Wild One, out."

Leroux removed his headset and tossed it on his workstation then rose.

"Why do you think he wanted to know where Jack is?" asked Tong as Leroux headed for the door.

He rolled his eyes. "I learned long ago not to ask questions I don't want to know the answer to."

Thorn Residence

Vienna, Austria

Jack—just Jack—stepped back inside after chuckling at one of his handler's neighbors struggling with his notorious British sports car that refused to start in the cold of an Austrian winter. He sat in one of the wingback chairs in Beverly Thorn's living room as she warmed herself by the fire. She was in pain. She was hiding it, but it was obvious. She had been brutalized by the Russian savages to within an inch of her life, and while the bruises had gone away and the bones had knit, she had never fully recovered.

She sat and he poured her a cup of tea then handed it to her. She smiled gratefully, cupping her hands around the hot brew. "Thank you. How do you feel about going back on duty?"

"Can't wait. It was nice to have a couple of weeks off, but I'm ready to get back in the game, assuming my exposure hasn't blown my cover."

"Langley's assessment is that it hasn't. If anything, it's solidified it. As a tacit thank you for our help, the Kremlin agreed to have your photo and any reference to you removed from all their news sites, and Langley's been scrubbing your image from anywhere they can and planting false stories with the same information, but a different man's image. You might not be able to get rid of something once it's out there, but you can drown it in a tsunami of crap that's almost as effective. If someone Googles your cover's name, they're going to find multiple faces associated with it, all tied to the same story, and you can claim if anyone challenges you that it was a case of mistaken identity. You just happen to look like the guy. If it becomes an issue, we'll either reassign you or retire you."

Jack groaned. "My God, don't retire me. I'm too damn young for that."

"I don't think it'll come to that. From what we can tell, the Russians actually believe you're an embassy worker in Warsaw who was framed. We have a situation in Belarus that needs your attention. Can you be there in two days?"

He shrugged. "Sure."

"Good. I've emailed you your briefing package. Familiarize yourself with it and if you have any questions, let me know."

"Will do." He leaned forward, putting his tea on the table. "Can I ask you a personal question?"

She regarded him. "I suppose. I don't promise an answer."

He chuckled. "Have you talked to anybody about your situation?"

"And what situation is that?"

"The fact you're in constant pain."

"If I talked to anybody, you know what they would do."

"Is retirement really so bad?"

"You tell me. If I was retired, I wouldn't have been able to help you."

"Oh, you would've still found a way, but I'm more concerned with you. Are you on painkillers?"

"Tylenol. Extra strength," she added with a smirk.

"That's not painkillers. You might as well be on Flintstone vitamins. I mean real painkillers."

She frowned. "I've considered it, but they can be highly addictive. I've seen the damage they can do."

"May I make a suggestion?"

"What's that?"

"Get the prescription and just take one a week. Even if you only get a few hours where you feel normal, that might end up doing wonders for you. And I promise, if I ever see you popping them like House, I'll kidnap you myself and put you in a facility."

She laughed. "I think you would."

His phone vibrated with a message and he checked to see it had come through the secure network. He logged in and his eyebrows shot up.

"Something wrong?"

He wagged his phone. "Dylan says he needs me in Warsaw ASAP. OTB."

Thorn eyed him. "Off the books? That's odd."

"With him, not so much." He rose. "If you'll excuse me, I've got a flight to catch." He waved her off as she began to stand. "I'll show myself out. You take care of yourself and consider what I said. Don't suffer because you're afraid of what might happen, when what is actually happening is making you miserable."

"Wise words, my young friend."

He grinned at her as he ran his hands down his body. "All this and brains too."

She giggled and batted a hand at him. "Get the hell out of here. Don't forget, I need you in Belarus in two days no matter what Kane needs you for."

"I'll be there, don't you worry."

Presidential Executive Office, The Kremlin

Moscow, Russia

Peskov sat behind his desk in his office, two of Nikitin's men setting up equipment for the expected phone call from Victor. The president had agreed to allow Nikitin to be read in, and once he realized what was truly going on, he had been furious at being kept out of the loop, listing a myriad of things done incorrectly, not the least of which was employing Firouz as the courier. But that was spilled vodka. It didn't matter anymore. What mattered was what they did next.

Victor had admitted he was the leak. That had been a shock, but no one, including the president, believed that the boy's father had put him up to it. It was a crime of opportunity, and the president had authorized the exchange—Victor for his family, for the young man was correct. His father's future in this country was over because of what had happened and the story they had put out earlier. The man's reputation was destroyed and the Kremlin couldn't admit to what was really going on, so they would act as if he were guilty and confiscate all of his assets and imprison him. The president was more concerned with containing the leak and placating the Chinese so the deal could go through.

The phone in the outer office rang and his secretary answered. "One moment, please." She poked her head through the door. "It's him."

Nikitin rose from his perch in the corner. "Are you ready?" His men nodded. "Put it through."

Peskov's secretary disappeared and Nikitin closed the door, but not before he dismissed the two men who weren't cleared to hear the conversation. The phone rang and Peskov picked it up, Nikitin listening in on an extension.

"Hello?"

"Hello, sir. It's Victor Stepanov."

"Yes, I've been expecting your call."

"Have you had time to consider my offer?"

"I have. And if you hand yourself over with the intel, we'll free your mother and your sisters, but not your father."

"That's not what we agreed to."

"We didn't agree to anything, son. You made a proposal. I'm telling you what we're willing to do. Hand yourself over with the intel and we'll set your mother and sisters free."

The line went dead, and Peskov cursed, hanging up the phone.

Nikitin regarded him. "Well, that was unexpected. Just when were you going to tell me you had changed the agreement?"

"I hadn't decided to until I heard his voice. He'll call back. It's a good deal."

"He'd be a fool to agree to it."

"Oh, it's negotiable. We'll put his mother and sisters on a plane and let him hand himself over after the fact. His father's the bargaining chip. It's believable we wouldn't want to let him go so easily."

"But I think we did learn something," said Nikitin.

"And what's that?"

"He's being advised."

Peskov's eyes narrowed. "How do you figure that?"

"He ended that call too quickly. Somebody told him to hang up. A twenty-two-year-old is going to panic in a situation like that. He's going to plead his case. Instead, he just hung up. He'll call back, like you said, but he's going to have a new position."

"Who's advising him?"

"It has to be the Americans."

"If he's with the Americans, then why are they letting this happen?"

"I think it's quite clear that he's already handed over the intel, so the Americans don't care. They're probably helping him out of the goodness of their own heart."

"If the Americans already know, then there's no point in this exchange. We're wasting our time here."

"No, you're forgetting one thing. Our aim here is to show him to the Chinese, to show them that we plugged the leak. If we bring him in, even if we have to release his family, we can show to them that the leak is plugged and the deal can go through. They don't need to know that the Americans are aware of what's going on. And if you want, as soon as we have him in custody, we can either terminate his family or bring them back, but we need to control him. He's the wild card."

Peskov's eyebrows shot up. "You're actually suggesting killing a woman and her two children on American soil?"

"No. Which is why the exchange has to happen somewhere else. And my guess is whoever's advising him has told him the same thing."

"If he's being advised, then why did he propose a flight to the United States in the first place?"

"Because I believe he's telling the truth. We know he was on a city bus and that he caused it to crash. I think he ran away from the Americans, then had second thoughts. I think that initial conversation was him on a phone that he borrowed, just like he said. I think in the past hour he's been picked back up by the Americans and the game has changed. You watch, he's going to call you back, agree to his mother and sisters being handed over, but he won't turn himself in until they're safe, and he'll propose Warsaw or someplace close, much closer than the United States."

"And if he does agree to it?"

"We'll make it clear that if he reneges, his father pays the price and that we'll track down his mother and sisters and make them pay as well. Remember, the entire goal here is to get him into custody as quickly as possible."

The intercom beeped and Peskov picked up the phone. "Yes?"

"It's him again."

"Put him through." The line flashed and he tapped it. "Hello, Victor. I take it you've had time to consider my offer?"

"Yes, and it's unacceptable."

"I'm open to a counterproposal."

"You set my mother and sisters free and put them on a plane to Warsaw. As soon as I hear from them that they're safe, I'll hand myself over."

Peskov leaned back, raising his hands in triumph. "How can I be certain that you haven't handed the intel over to the Americans?"

"I haven't. I swear."

"I'll tell you what, Victor, I'm going to give you the benefit of the doubt. I'm going to order the release of your mother and your sisters, and have them put on the first flight to Warsaw. When they arrive there, they'll call you, and you'll have thirty minutes to hand yourself in. If you renege on your end of the deal, not only will I track down your family and bring them back here, but I promise your father will be beaten day in and day out for the rest of his life. And if I ever get my hands on you, the same will happen to you. Do you understand me?"

The terror of understanding was clear in Victor's voice. "I-I understand, sir."

"Very well. Then we have a deal?"

"Yes, sir."

"Call me back in thirty minutes and I'll let you know what flight your family's on."

"Yes, sir."

Peskov ended the call and Nikitin got on his phone. "Report." He listened, grunting several times, then hung up. "He's lying."

"What do you mean he's lying?"

"Voice stress analyzer says he was lying when he said he hadn't given the intel to the Americans."

Peskov cursed. "Now what do we do?"

"We honor the deal. Remember, our goal here is to get our hands on him. Whether he already handed the intel over to the Americans is inconsequential with respect to that goal. However, now that we know the Americans know exactly what this is about, we have to expect they're going to attempt to interfere."

"What could they possibly do beyond rattle their sabers like they always do? It's their ultimate weakness. All they do is talk, talk, talk. In the meantime, we act. Let's get the three of them on a plane to Warsaw immediately, and have people on the ground there ready to pick them up the moment we have Victor in custody. I'm going to talk to the president. If this deal's going to go through, it has to go through in sooner than forty-eight hours. We need to start rolling the assets to the Chinese border. The moment the Chinese agree the deal's back on, I want those nukes on their side of the border, and then it's too late for the Americans to do anything."

Nikitin smirked. "Oh, I'm sure they'll still be talking."

CIA Safe House
Moscow, Russia

Kane watched Victor shaking like a leaf as he headed up the stairs to his room. He felt sorry for the kid. He was in an impossible situation that no 22-year-old should ever have to face. Washington had indicated it was unlikely the president would be contacting Moscow or Beijing until the morning, Moscow time. It gave Victor's mother and sister plenty of time to reach Warsaw, then disappear with the help of Jack and Warsaw Station.

The question now was how to save Victor. That would be easy if the young man's free will was taken out of the equation. They would simply put him into the underground railroad and get him out of the country rather than have him hand himself over. Kane wasn't a father, but he had to imagine any father, including Victor's, would rather suffer what Victor faced, than have his own son be tortured in his place.

Sherrie descended the stairs then sat beside him.

"How's he doing?"

She frowned. "About as well as can be expected, I guess. Langley just confirmed that the mother and sisters are on board the flight. It lands in two hours."

Kane tapped his ear. "I got the same update. Jack will be on the ground in an hour and Warsaw Station is ready."

"What do you think will happen?"

"My guess is they'll renege on the terms of the deal."

Her eyes narrowed. "What do you mean?"

"I mean, there's no way they're on that plane alone, and they'll be met on the ground as well. I'm guessing they won't be allowed to leave until they have Victor and the intel in their hands."

"That would make sense. So, what are we going to do?"

Kane chewed his cheek, slowly shaking his head. "There's not much we can do. It's a reasonable precaution on their part, and we can't exactly start blowing away Russian government agents on Polish soil."

"What if they renege after Victor hands himself over and they try to take his family back to Moscow?"

"That's when we can intervene. It'll ruffle Polish feathers, but one call from the White House will settle that down, especially once things become public about what's actually happening." He sighed. "I'm worried about the kid. How do you weigh the value of a life? If he doesn't hand himself over, his mother and sisters could be imprisoned and tortured, perhaps executed, his father certainly. If he does, then his mother and sisters live, and perhaps even his father."

"You're not thinking of trying to rescue him, are you?"

Kane smirked. "The thought had crossed my mind, though how we'd accomplish it, I'm not sure."

"We?"

He grinned. "I figured you'd want in."

"Oh, you know I want in. It's just that I'd like to be able to get out as well."

"Then we've got some serious scheming to do."

Operations Center 3, CIA Headquarters

Langley, Virginia

Leroux rubbed his eyes and yawned. Because of the seriousness of what was going on, the operation was compartmentalized to his team only. No relief. Earlier in the day, he had started switching off team members, one-third for four hours at a time. He, unfortunately, had only managed a couple of hours the night before. He was exhausted, but it was his girlfriend and his best friend out there, and things kept happening that needed his attention.

It was times like these that he wished he had never given up his Red Bull habit.

The door to the operations center opened and Sonya Tong entered, earlier than scheduled.

He tapped his watch. "Shouldn't you be sleeping?"

She shrugged. "I got a couple of hours, and don't forget, I got four hours this morning, so I'm actually feeling pretty good. You, on the other hand, need to get some sleep. I can handle things here."

She was right. She could handle things, but so much was happening over the next few hours that he didn't want to miss anything.

She sat at her station and faced him. "They're not landing in Warsaw for two more hours, so nothing should happen between now and then. Go get some rack time, and if anything does happen, I'll wake you up personally."

Something stirred below at the memory of the last time she had woken him personally, when in the dark he had thought she was Sherrie and they had exchanged a passionate kiss. He blasted air between his lips, then rose. "You're right. If anything happens, wake me. But stay at your post. Send Randy." He flashed her a wink. "No matter how dark it is, there'll be no misunderstanding."

She giggled and he headed for the door, his entire body already shutting down in anticipation of hitting one of the beds in the temporary quarters meant for situations just like this.

Child cleared his throat. "Um, I got something."

Leroux stopped but Tong beat him to the punch. "Is it life or death?"

"Err, no."

She turned to Leroux. "Go. I'll brief you in two hours."

She was right. He was in no condition to deal with anything anymore, and he continued out the door, already half asleep and completely useless.

Warsaw Chopin Airport
Warsaw, Poland

"Men's bathroom on your left, far stall on the left. As soon as you enter, they'll leave your care package hanging on the stall door."

Jack suppressed a smile at the sultry voice of Sonya Tong in his ear. God, he wanted to meet her someday. She sounded gorgeous, and there was no doubt she was brilliant. She had even displayed a healthy sense of humor. But what was he thinking? Relationships weren't for him, at least nothing that lasted beyond an assignment. To him, a long-term relationship was someone he saw once or twice a year and did the nasty with. Friends with benefits, quite often enemies with benefits. They both got what they needed out of it—a good time. He always treated them right, he always cared for them in the moment, but each side of the equation understood there was no commitment, no obligations, no expectations. A woman like Tong would expect much more, and deservedly so. She would remain a fantasy, never to be fulfilled.

And that was fun in itself.

He didn't respond to Tong's update. Talking to yourself was one good way to appear suspicious. He entered the bathroom to find half a dozen people inside, most at the sinks, the rest at the urinals. The stall door at the far end opened and a man stepped out. Jack gave him a friendly nod and stepped into the vacated stall, closing the door and locking it. On the back of the door, as promised, was a black duffel bag. He relieved himself, since he didn't know when he would get his next chance, then opened the bag. He retrieved a Glock and three mags, plus a fresh set of embassy credentials giving him diplomatic immunity should things go to shit. He retrieved a few more tools of the trade that would allow him to bypass most of the security doors within the airport, then body armor disguised as a regular vest. He zipped the bag up and hung it on the back of the door, then put on his armor. He flushed the toilet, counted to ten, then opened the door, heading for the sinks.

His supplier rushed in, heading for the stall and grabbing the bag off the back of the door. "I can't believe I forgot this," he muttered to no one in particular, disappearing as quickly as he had appeared.

Jack washed his hands as Tong cooed in his ear. "That went smooth. Your target's flight is arriving in forty-five minutes. So far, it's on schedule. I suggest you get yourself a coffee and find a quiet corner. When you leave the bathroom, the food court is to your left, two-minute walk."

Jack dried his hands, heading for the food court, though he had no intention of getting a coffee. The last thing he needed was a diuretic when on an op. He spotted some golden arches and his stomach rumbled. He hadn't eaten since breakfast. Perhaps it was time to take care of that problem as well.

Quarter pounder combo coming up.

Operations Center 3, CIA Headquarters

Langley, Virginia

Leroux entered the operations center feeling a little more himself. He had dropped to sleep the moment his head hit the pillow, and he was convinced it might have actually been a few seconds before that. He arranged for the attendant on duty to wake him in exactly two hours, and they had. It wasn't much sleep, but it was valuable sleep, and would hopefully carry him through the next phase of the operation.

"Report," he said as he headed for his station, staring at the displays.

Tong filled him in. "The plane's just landed in Warsaw and is disembarking now."

He pointed at the display. "Feed?"

"Number one. We should be able to see them any moment now."

"Run everyone's face. We need to know who their escorts are."

"Already on it."

He dropped in his chair. "I knew I could leave things in your capable hands."

She flashed him a smile. "Always." She resumed. "Jack's in place to intercept them in the International Arrivals area. We have embassy officials on site with the visas, and the Oval Office is ready to make a call should it become necessary."

"We're going to have to assume the Russians are armed and that they bypassed security in Moscow. Make sure Jack is aware."

"He is."

"And Moscow?"

"They're in position for the handover, but Kane's up to something."

Leroux groaned. "What?"

"He wouldn't say, but he did ask for a special delivery from Moscow Station."

"Do we have any idea what he's up to?"

"He's activated the underground railroad. A team's in place. They've been told to expect a delivery within five minutes of the exchange. It's all very confusing. I'm only getting bits and pieces from Chief of Station Moscow. She says she's too damn busy to explain things and that I can read her report when it's done."

Leroux stared at the ceiling. "Wonderful. Who needs sleep when you can just worry yourself to death?"

Krymsky Bridge
Moscow, Russia

Peskov stood in the frigid cold. The little bastard had called at the last minute and changed the deal. Only he and Victor's father were allowed at the meet. He had been about to refuse when Nikitin had waved him off, giving him a thumbs-up, later explaining that sniper teams would be set up to make sure he didn't get away. They were both convinced that the Americans were up to something. Most likely, they would grab Victor and his father and make a break for it.

"My son will not show. He's no fool."

Peskov glanced at Alexei Stepanov. "Your son has indicated he's already on the way. Your wife and daughters' lives depend on it."

"You're a monster."

"What would *you* do if he weren't your son and had betrayed your country, putting its very future at risk?"

Alexei frowned. "So, he is to die?"

"Yes, a crime like his can't go unpunished. If you knew what was going on, you would realize how grave an error in judgment he made."

A car approached, stopping midway on the bridge. His phone rang and he answered it. It was Victor.

"I'm here. Let me speak to my mother."

"You'll get a call in a moment."

Peskov ended the call then dialed Nikitin. "Have her make the call."

"Yes, sir."

Alexei glared at him. "If you lay a finger on them, I swear you'll die a horrible death."

Peskov sneered at him. "You're hardly in any position to make threats."

"We'll see about that."

Warsaw Chopin Airport

Warsaw, Poland

Jack watched as a terrified Maria Stepanov took the phone handed her by one of the four escorts Langley had identified. The woman had obviously been informed of what was going on, and the strangled conversation with her son was heartbreaking to witness. He eyed his targets should things go south. Their visible escorts were two burly men, experienced FSB agents, according to Langley. The other two were pretending to be a couple seated nearby, kissing and getting into it a little too much for them to be paying proper attention.

He would take them out last.

"Jackrabbit, Control. He's just told her to look for you."

Jack rose, disappointed it was Leroux in his ear again, and strode toward the terrified family. He smiled pleasantly at the woman and her daughters then turned to the one clearly in charge. "Are we good?"

The man regarded him with disdain. "American pig. I should shoot you where you stand."

"Where's the fun in that? If you kill me, my partner will have all four of you down before you even spot him."

Both men backed off slightly, their heads on swivels, searching for Jack's imaginary partner.

"Now, how about we park the attitude and just do our jobs?" He tapped his ear. "I assume you're receiving instructions. Are they good to go?"

The man frowned, turning away, someone from Moscow obviously listening in. He nodded and turned back a moment later without having said anything. "We're good."

"Thank you." Jack held out an arm, beckoning Victor's family. "Let's go."

Maria put an arm around both her daughters and followed Jack toward the doors, tears streaming down all their cheeks when Leroux's voice came in over his ear. "Watch your back, Jack. Something's going on in Moscow."

South of Krymsky Bridge

Moscow, Russia

Sherrie peered through the scope of her sniper rifle supplied by Moscow Station less than an hour ago. Drones had been deployed with infrared cameras, and two sniper teams had been spotted on rooftops on opposite ends of the bridge. Kane's plan was insane, and it was going to get somebody killed if they couldn't take out the sniper teams should it become necessary.

"I'm in position," reported Larry over her earpiece.

"Copy that. So am I. Don't take the shot until I give the order."

"Roger that. Standing by."

Peskov stepped forward and was handed the memory card, saying something she couldn't hear. He appeared satisfied with the nodded response, then held his phone to his ear.

And all hell broke loose.

"Take the shot!"

Krymsky Bridge
Moscow, Russia

Kane cursed at Peskov's words.

"I've got the intel. Get the family back."

Kane fell back toward the car, the mask of Victor's face having fooled everyone so far.

"If you try to run, Victor, you'll die, and so will your family."

Alexei roared in rage and stormed toward Peskov as the clap of two sniper rifles echoed across the bridge from opposite directions, quickly followed by two more shots.

"Sniper Team One eliminated," reported Sherrie.

"Sniper Team Two eliminated," confirmed Larry.

Kane continued to fall back toward his car. He drew his weapon just in case there were others in hiding that Langley hadn't spotted, but held his fire. He had no desire to kill the Russian Chief of Staff.

Alexei raised his cuffed hands over his head then reached out and dropped his arms behind Peskov's back, squeezing him in a bear hug. "Run, son, run!"

Kane's heart ached that the man was sacrificing himself for a complete stranger, that his son was already in the underground railroad, but he held his tongue, maintaining his cover. Alexei lifted Peskov off the ground, carrying him toward the edge of the bridge. Peskov screamed in terror as he realized what was happening, and punched at the barrel of a man to no avail.

Alexei twisted his head toward Kane and their eyes met. "I love you all!"

And with that, they disappeared over the side, Peskov's blood-curdling scream falling silent the moment they hit the icy waters below. Kane jumped in the car and hammered on the gas, pulling a 180 then speeding from the area.

"Control, Wild One. Leave a drone behind to see if you can spot any survivors. Sniper teams, head for your respective switch points. Control, watch for any additional surveillance, over."

"Roger that, Wild One. So far you look clear all the way to Switch Point Alpha."

"What's the status in Warsaw?"

"Stand by, Wild One. It's still in progress."

Kane didn't like the sound of that.

183

Warsaw Chopin Airport
Warsaw, Poland

"Stop."

Jack cursed as his comms squawked in his ears. "Things have gone south in Moscow," reported Leroux.

Jack whipped around, drawing his weapon, and put two in the leader's chest, then two more in his partner's before diving to his right and rolling to a knee as the fake couple reacted, both with their weapons out far faster than he had expected. The man was aiming at him, but the woman was aiming at the girls.

Jack made a split-second decision and squeezed off two more rounds. The woman dropped, her gun thundering as her body shook. Her partner fired off two rounds and Jack winced as he took two on the right side of his chest. He fell backward and released his weapon, grabbing it with his left hand as he hit the ground. He found his target preparing to fire again, and squeezed the trigger, putting a hole through the man's neck. His target dropped to his knees then aimed at the family. Jack fired three more rounds, the man shaking with each impact before collapsing, dead.

Jack sprawled on the floor as shouts closed in on his position. His head lolled to the side and he smiled at the sight of the mother huddled against the door with her two daughters, her arm bleeding from a graze, but alive.

"Jackrabbit, Control. Are you all right?"

Jack lay flat and tossed his weapon as far as he could so the arriving airport security didn't shoot him on sight.

"Jackrabbit, what's your status?"

He groaned then reached over and released one of the Velcro straps on the bulletproof vest. "Two in the vest. I should live."

"Embassy personnel are almost at your position. Just stand by. We'll get you out of there eventually."

"Eventually? Not sure I like the sound of that."

South of Krymsky Bridge

Moscow, Russia

Kane started the engine of the tiny Nissan Micra and pulled out of the parking spot in the underground garage, the tinted windows protecting against prying eyes, and Langley's hack of the cameras everything else. He pulled out onto the street as a helicopter thundered overhead, heading toward the scene of the crime. The Russians weren't going to react well to this, but it was rather poetic—the Russian president's most senior advisor killed by one of his greatest allies, all in the name of saving his son, a son who was already saved.

Kane had always assumed he would die on the job, though his lack of concern over that had faded over the years since he met Fang. He would prefer to live to a ripe old age by her side, perhaps with a couple of children and even more grandchildren. Dying for your country was one thing. If he did, he would be honored to have his star engraved on the memorial wall at CIA Headquarters. But if he did go, he hoped it would be like Victor's father, sacrificing himself to save the ones he loved.

He ran a knuckle over his misty eyes and activated his comms. "Control, Wild One, come in, over."

"This is Control."

"Control, any sign of pursuit?"

"Negative, looks like you're clear."

"And the others?"

"Everyone successfully made their first exchange points."

"What's the status on Victor?"

"He's already reached the third transfer point. He's deep in. We should have him out of the city by morning."

"And his family?"

"That situation's in flux. Jack took out the four escorts, but took two rounds in the vest. He'll be okay. The Polish authorities are on scene now, and the embassy officials are dealing with it. The White House is making a call to try to smooth things over."

"Good. Keep me posted. Now, put me through to Victor."

"Repeat that."

"Put me through to Victor. There's something he needs to know."

"Negative, Wild One. He's incommunicado. Once he's out the other end of the railroad, I can connect you."

Kane exhaled with frustration but understood the precautions. He had had a hell of a time convincing Victor to do the switch in the first place, but had convinced him it was the only chance they had of possibly freeing his father, and that history suggested there was no way the Russian president could be trusted—his father was going to die regardless, and the only people who could really be saved were his mother and sisters, and himself if he would allow it. It wasn't until Larry had sat Victor down and told him how as a father, he would never want his son to do what Victor was about to do, and that he would sacrifice himself in a heartbeat if it meant saving his child, that Victor listened. Larry's words had turned the tide, and proved prescient.

the Russian president could be trusted—his father was going to die regardless, and the only people who could really be saved were his mother and sisters, and himself if he would allow it. It wasn't until Larry had sat Victor down and told him how as a father, he would never want his son to do what Victor was about to do, and that he would sacrifice himself in a heartbeat if it meant saving his child, that Victor listened. Larry's words had turned the tide, and proved prescient.

"Wild One, Control. We've got an update for you."

"Go ahead."

"We've got drone footage showing Peskov climbing out of the water."

Kane cursed. "The bastard's alive?"

"Affirmative. EMTs are with him now. Looks like they had more eyes on the place."

Kane sighed. "Any sign of Victor's father?"

"Negative. We'll keep looking, but he was handcuffed. I can't see him making it."

Kane had to agree. Surviving a plunge into frigid waters was one thing, doing it handcuffed was something entirely different. He was just disappointed that the man's final act of love had failed.

Warsaw Chopin Airport
Warsaw, Poland

Jack sat with the two sisters as their mother was tended to by paramedics. She had been grazed by the lone bullet aimed in their direction, using her body to shield her daughters. It was minor and she would be fine, and she would only need a dressing for a few days. There was certainly nothing that would prevent her from getting on the flight they had scheduled to the US. The deputy chief of mission from the embassy was in discussions with increasingly more senior Polish officials, government representatives having just arrived, the head of airport security and the airport itself not senior enough to deal with the situation.

"Did it hurt?" asked the youngest daughter, Alina.

He smiled at her. "Yep, but not too bad. It'll be an ugly bruise, but it'll go away. Just like your mom's cut."

"Will she be all right?" asked the older sister, Inessa.

"Absolutely. Unless she doesn't eat her vegetables, then her arm might fall off."

Alina's eyes bulged and Inessa giggled. "He's joking," she said, admonishing her sister with a swat on the arm.

"Ow."

"What's going to happen to us?"

"You're going to go to America where you'll be safe."

"What about our father?" asked Alina.

Jack had already received the report on the man's fate, but it wasn't his place to tell these children that they would never see their father again. "We'll have to see what happens. But just know this, your father loves you, and all he cares about is making sure you and your mother and your brother are safe."

"What's happened with Victor?" asked Inessa, her eyes wide. "They said horrible things about him."

Jack smiled at her, gently patting her hand. "The people who said those things were bad people, that's why your father and your brother wanted you to get to safety. Your brother will be with you soon."

Both girls brightened at this revelation. "Really? When?" asked Inessa.

Jack chuckled. "I can't give you an exact date and time, but soon, probably in the next few days. And when this is all over, when you and your family are safe, don't forget to ask your brother what he did to help save the world."

Alina's eyes bulged. "He saved the world?"

Jack punched her on the chin gently. "Your brother's a superhero." He noticed the deputy chief walking toward him, the negotiations apparently complete. "Excuse me, girls." He rose and joined him. "What's the word?"

"They're pissed."

"No shit."

"Oh, you don't realize how pissed they are. They want you up on murder charges."

"Self defense."

"They don't care, but fortunately for you, your forged diplomatic papers give you diplomatic immunity, and the president himself just vouched for you. The call just came through now from their president's office."

"Bottom line it for me."

"They want you out of the country right away. Your credentials have been revoked."

Jack grinned. "Can't revoke what you don't have."

"Well, keep that to yourself."

"And the Stepanovs?"

"They're free to go. As far as the Poles are concerned, they were never officially in Polish territory because they never cleared the international transit area. Their flight leaves in thirty minutes and you'll be on it with them."

"I don't think so. Stateside isn't in my plans. I've got an op in less than two days where I need to be east of here, shall we say."

The deputy chief frowned. "I don't know what to tell you. They want you on that flight and they don't give a shit."

Jack sighed. "I need to hit the head."

"Are you going to cause me more headaches?"

Jack grinned. "Probably."

"Go ahead. Just try not to kill anybody else."

"I make no promises."

Operations Center 3, CIA Headquarters

Langley, Virginia

Leroux squinted at the security camera footage as a man stepped out of the bathroom in the international arrivals area at the Warsaw airport. "Is that Jack?"

Everyone leaned forward, staring at the screen. Tong tapped at her keyboard and zoomed in on the man as he walked in the opposite direction of the earlier incident, pushing a maintenance cart and wearing a janitor's uniform. Leroux groaned as all doubt was removed when the image expanded. It was definitely Jack.

Child spun in his chair, laughing. "You know what that means?"

Leroux was afraid to ask. "What? That there's some innocent Polish janitor unconscious in a bathroom stall?"

"No, that there's a naked janitor unconscious in a bathroom stall."

Tong giggled. "Well, let's hope he didn't take his underwear."

Leroux sighed. "Monitor him. Let's make sure he gets out safely. He's got an op in Belarus in thirty-six hours that he can't be late for."

He turned to Tong. "Now, before all this excitement, you had mentioned some progress on our search."

Tong nodded. Turning back to her station, she brought up several data intercepts and transcripts of conversations picked up by Echelon. "We were able to identify the container type that's being used to transport the missile systems. We intercepted requisition orders for fifty containers seven days ago, all to be delivered to eight different sites."

"Just eight?"

"Yes, there might be another order out there for the other sites we thought might be involved, but this is what we found."

"And how many went to Chkalovsky Air Base?"

"Twelve. It's the biggest shipment, and Kane saw six of them."

"So, the other six are in one of the other buildings?"

"In building number three, actually." She brought up some satellite footage showing the containers arriving by rail and being offloaded with a crane. "This is three days ago."

"Any footage of more launchers arriving?"

"Negative. We're still going back, but it looks like they were already inside. Watch what happens when they offload one of these things." She sped up the footage and Leroux stood, his arms folded as he watched the crane reposition the front of the container near the rear door.

"Do we have a better angle?"

"No. Unfortunately, the satellite's directly overhead so we can't see what's happening inside, but see that black smoke coming out the door?"

Leroux smiled. "Diesel."

"Exactly. I think they're backing the launcher into the container from inside the warehouse." She sped the video forward some more, and he watched as the container was pulled inside, revealing rollers embedded in the ground that no doubt continued inside, a motorized winch system doing the work.

He sat. "Okay, that explains twelve of them, thirty-eight to go."

"We have footage of similar activity happening at the other seven facilities. If we're dealing with fifty, then we've identified where they're all coming from."

"And does it look like they're all going out by rail?"

"Yes."

"Thank God for small miracles."

"What do you mean?" asked Child, dropping his foot and killing his customary spin.

"Well, if they loaded these things in the back of some Antonovs, the Russians could fly them straight into Beijing, and the only way we'd be able to stop them is to blow them out of the sky, which would be a pretty blatant act of war. If they took them by road, they have hundreds of possible routes they could take, but by rail, there are only two lines that connect Russia and China."

Child's eyebrows shot up. "Only two?"

"Yep. And one of them goes through Mongolia, so there's no way they'll risk using that."

"So, what are we going to do?"

"That's a question left to the Pentagon and the White House. We've done our job. We've found the damn things. What's done about it is up to people who get paid a hell of a lot more than we do."

Presidential Executive Office, The Kremlin
Moscow, Russia

Peskov still trembled from his ordeal. He wasn't sure how much of it was from the cold and how much from fear. He should be dead. It was pure luck that he wasn't. When they had hit the water, he had somehow cut through the surface quicker, freeing himself of Alexei's bear hug. He had managed to kick away and reached the shore despite the best efforts of the current of the Moskva River. Fortunately, there were security teams positioned all around the area, and the drone operator monitoring the exchange had followed him rather than Victor. Nikitin would say it had been a mistake, but he would tell the man to go to hell. He was alive because of it, otherwise, he would have frozen on the shore.

He was dried off now, in comfortable clothes, buried in heated blankets, with piping hot tea gripped in his hands that he slowly nursed through chattering teeth.

His secretary regarded him with concern. "Are you sure there's nothing else I can get you?"

"No, I'll be fine. I just need time to warm up. If I ever make fun of the Polar Bear Club again, you remind me of this."

She laughed. "Well, at least you didn't lose your sense of humor, sir."

He grunted. "I wasn't aware I had one."

She smiled. "You do." She jerked her chin toward the door. "Director Nikitin is outside and would like to see you if you're up to it."

"Send him in." He took another sip of his tea and Nikitin appeared in the doorway a moment later.

"How are you feeling?"

"Like a damn penguin."

Nikitin laughed. "Do penguins feel the cold?"

"A plucked one does."

Nikitin roared. "This is definitely one for the books. Too bad we can never tell anybody about it."

"True. Any luck finding Victor?"

"No. We managed to track his car to a nearby parking garage, but there was no sign of him. It looks like it was well-coordinated, likely by the Americans. If he's in their underground railroad, we'll never see him again."

Peskov cursed. "The Chinese aren't going to be happy about that."

"No, but I had a thought."

"What?"

"We have young men his age coming back from the front constantly. We just need to take one that generally matches his description, someone who's had his face blown off, take some photos, say it's him and that he died in a shootout. Show the video of the exchange. That should prove the father was the motivator. He's dead, the son's dead, we get this deal going."

Peskov considered the idea for a moment. He didn't mind lying to the Russian people. That was part of the job. The masses didn't know what was good for them, and usually couldn't handle the truth. But to lie to the Chinese? If they were to find out, the consequences could be grave. He sighed. "I don't think we have a choice. Make it happen, and make it happen fast. I want the evidence in Beijing's hands before morning. Anything else I need to know?"

"Yes. The family got away."

"What? How the hell did that happen?"

"The Americans had an agent at the airport. He managed to take out all four of our people. We've confirmed that the mother and children are on a flight to New York as we speak."

"Can we intercept?"

Nikitin regarded him. "Yes. But we won't."

Peskov cocked an eyebrow. "We won't?"

"No. To take out women and children on American soil isn't worth the diplomatic cost."

Peskov cursed. Nikitin was right. They couldn't create a diplomatic incident like that, not with everything going on. Besides, it was over. Alexei Stepanov was dead. His spouse and children, with the exception of Victor, were irrelevant. And if Victor were indeed in the underground railroad, he was lost to them. Their only hope would be to watch for him to slip up, and perhaps a year from now, or ten, justice could be served. But for now, the world needed to believe that Victor was dead.

"There's nothing we can do about them now. They're irrelevant. Stage his death. Put together a package for the Chinese. It's time to focus on the deal. Is the president in?"

"No, he's gone home and is in bed."

Peskov glanced at the clock on the wall. "Did he leave instructions?"

"Only one."

Peskov tensed. "And that was?"

"To not screw this up."

Operations Center 3, CIA Headquarters
Langley, Virginia

Leroux rose, still exhausted, as Morrison entered the operations center, his boss' usual pep nowhere to be found.

"Report."

Leroux pointed at the displays. "Sir, ten minutes ago we observed activity at eight separate Russian installations. The containers that we believe are being used to transport the missile systems are being loaded onto railcars as we speak."

"And we still think there are fifty of them?"

"Yes, sir. It matches up with the conversation Kane had with Peskov. They were promising delivery of fifty systems starting within forty-eight hours, we have an intercepted requisition for fifty of these exact shipping containers, and photographic proof from Kane that three of these containers were loaded with the mobile launchers, so we have to assume all fifty are."

"When will they be rolling?"

"These are big and heavy. So far, our estimates are twenty minutes per container. Some of the sites only have four or five to load, so in less than two hours we could have trains heading to China."

"Earliest arrival?"

"Sir, if the nearest base loads its six systems within two hours, in as little as twelve more hours they could be crossing the border into China."

Morrison cursed. "And once they do, there's no stopping this deal."

"How the hell are we supposed to stop it anyway?" cried Child in frustration. "I mean, what can we do? Scold them into not making the deal?"

Morrison turned toward the youngest member of the team. "That's a good question, son. And I can guarantee you everyone from the White House on down is trying to figure out exactly how to stop two countries who don't give a shit about international treaties from making the most dangerous weapons deal in history. If the Chinese get their hands on a significant portion of the Russian nuclear arsenal, there's nothing we can do to challenge them. They could roll straight across most of Asia if they wanted to, unopposed."

"Because Americans won't die for people who don't look like them?"

"I'm American," said Tong, one of two people in the room of Chinese descent.

"You know what I mean," said Child. "In World War Two, we went to war against the Nazis, because that's where the bulk of our ancestors came from. Western Europe. And we went to war in the Pacific because the Japanese attacked us. Are we going to go to war with China to save countries that barely any of our population calls their ancestral home if the Chinese don't attack us directly?"

Morrison frowned. "I don't know the answer to that, but I would hope in the past eighty years we've moved beyond using the color of our skin to determine who is worth fighting and dying for, and that we're now at the point where we realize all people, no matter where they live, deserve freedom and dignity. Unfortunately, we don't live in an ideal world, and I don't want to give the world a chance to answer your question, because I fear we'd both be disappointed in the result."

Morrison returned his attention to the main displays. "Keep feeding me estimates every thirty minutes. I want to know when each site has finished loading, when they get underway, and what's our best guess for reaching the Chinese border. And brief Kane. He has a way of thinking outside the box that the paper pushers at the Pentagon don't. I just have a funny feeling we'll be asking him to save us from our own indecision before the day is out."

CIA Safe House
Moscow, Russia

Kane tapped on Sherrie's bedroom door. "Come in," she called.

He opened the door and stepped inside. "Ah, darn, you're decent."

She gave him a look. "Well, it's not like you're only wearing a loincloth."

He chuckled and sat on the edge of her bed. "I just got off with Chris."

"Did you now? So, he's stepping out on me?"

Kane snickered. "Okay, I walked into that one. I just got off a *call* with your boyfriend, and Morrison's asked us to think outside the box."

"Let me guess. The Chief's concerned that the White House is just going to talk."

"Well, Chris is too polite to say it, at least on a monitored channel, but that's my guess."

"So, what's the lowdown?"

"Eight sites spread across the country, fifty weapons systems in total loaded into fifty containers loaded onto fifty railcars and eight different trains. Earliest arrival is estimated at approximately fourteen hours from now, the latest five days, and that's our monster, twelve weapon systems from Chkalovsky Air Base."

"Are the tags you placed still working?"

"Yes."

"What are you thinking?"

"I wanted to get your opinion."

Sherrie propped herself up against the headboard. "Well, my understanding is they've got two choke points. There are only two lines between Russia and China, one of which goes through Mongolia, so I doubt they'll use it."

"Agreed. And?"

"Blow the other one up."

Kane smiled. It was exactly what he was thinking. They couldn't touch anything on the Chinese side of the border until the missiles arrived. The Chinese technically hadn't done anything wrong. Then once they had, it would be an act of war with a country America did not want to get into a fight with, especially if its nuclear arsenal was multiplying rapidly due to the deal. Hit the Russian side of things, it might still be an act of war, but from a diplomatic perspective, it would be a justified attack. And if they just took out the rail line, it would be the proverbial slap on the wrist. Take out the actual trains, and you were destroying not only expensive weapons systems, but you were killing Russian personnel. "I like how you think."

"Do you think Washington will actually give the order?"

Kane frowned. "I don't think so. Things are happening too fast."

"So, what are you thinking?"

"Well, you're right. There are only two rail lines from Russia to China and one of them, the Trans-Mongolian, goes through Mongolia. There's no way in hell they're going to want to use that one for obvious reasons, so they're going to use the Trans-Siberian that bypasses Mongolia and enters China directly from the far eastern border. I say we get our asses out of Moscow and take out that railroad. That will at least buy the president some time. It'll bottleneck everything. And if they then decide to transport by road, they're going to have a hell of a time offloading those beasts without the proper equipment."

"So, are we doing this against orders?"

Kane smirked. "We're operations officers. Our job is to act independently and go wherever in the world we think we need to go to deal with threats to our country. Right now, there's nothing to do in Moscow. Victor's out. So is his family. His father's dead. We already have the only intel available. We've got the proof of the missile systems at the base and we've tagged several of them. They're being loaded on a train and will start rolling in less than two hours. Unless Langley wants us to go into the Kremlin and do some snooping, our job here is done. Everything we're trying to prevent is rolling east. So I say we get on a plane, get ahead of those trains, and at least be in position should the order be given. If we can take out the tracks ourselves, rather than the Pentagon having to call in an airstrike, it's a much less aggressive act of war."

"And if they still don't give the order?"

"We exercise operational independence."

She climbed out of the bed. "Then what are we waiting for?"

Presidential Executive Office, The Kremlin

Moscow, Russia

Peskov read the original English message received from the Americans less than half an hour ago, then the official Russian translation provided only moments ago. He was fluent in both languages, though there were nuances to each that could be lost in translation, and he preferred to rely on the original whenever possible, though even then, because he didn't grow up within the culture, some things were lost on him. It was one of the reasons why diplomatic messages were worded so carefully. A turn of phrase in one language could be completely misinterpreted in another.

Though there was no misinterpreting this.

The Americans were irate. At least a dozen treaty violations were listed, and they indicated that if the trains didn't reverse direction before reaching the border, not only would they be going public at the UN later today with all the evidence, immediate sanctions would be imposed, far more crippling than those already in place, and would include China.

Nikitin entered his office, holding up a folder. "I take it you've read this?"

Peskov tapped his own copy. "Rereading it."

Nikitin sat. "It's disheartening how large the security failure has been on this. From what I can tell, they've identified every single train, every single weapons system, and were even able to give serial numbers. They knew of Firouz's involvement, when the letter was handed over, when the response was received, what that response was. They might as well have had somebody sitting at the table the entire time being spoon-fed everything they needed to know."

Peskov couldn't disagree. It had been an abject failure, though who could have planned for the idealistic young son of a party loyalist and a birthday celebration that went far too late? It was the unexpected, the out-of-the-ordinary, the tiniest of details that caused the largest of operations to fail. How was Enigma cracked in World War II? Because every message ended with "Heil Hitler." The unbreakable code became breakable because of that one small screw-up, and here the biggest deal his country had ever brokered was threatened because of a birthday party.

He sighed, shaking the pages of the American communique. "There is one good thing here."

Nikitin cocked an eyebrow. "Oh?"

"All it is, is talk, talk, talk. They can have their emergency session at the UN today and that'll be more talk, then they can bring in sanctions against us and China. But as long as they just keep talking, those missiles are still moving. And by this evening our time, the first batch will cross the border, sealing the deal."

"And what if the Chinese decide not to proceed?"

"That's the question, isn't it? We have to assume Beijing received a similar communique. We'll have to see what they say, but they think long term, and economic sanctions might mean little to them if they establish the trading bloc they hope to with their Belt and Road initiative."

Nikitin's head bobbed. "Exactly as we predicted in our analysis five years ago. Honduras just the other day broke off all diplomatic relations with Taiwan after having received massive investments from the Chinese initiative. If they have sanctions brought in against them, they're going to start calling in their favors. And America could be in for a surprise when the airports and seaports paid for by Chinese Yuan deny US airlines and flagged vessels access. The Chinese have been planning for this for years, but they've never had the military clout to pull the trigger. As soon as they have our weapons, they will. My guess is the Chinese will deny any knowledge, claim the message young Victor says he translated is a fake, then privately indicate to us that the deal proceeds if we can get the weapons across the border. At least that's what I think will happen. But what do I know? I've only been doing this for forty years."

Peskov chuckled. "Let's hope you're right. We need this deal. Otherwise, I fear for our country's future."

Nikitin firmly disagreed. "I don't. We've made it this far without Chinese money, and while we may struggle in the short term, I prefer to think long term like the Chinese do. In the end, our country will adapt, our people will overcome, and we'll be stronger than ever before. We just have to be patient. It's deals like this that can have unintended consequences, and those can be far more dangerous than the gun already pointed at your head."

Peskov regarded the man. "I take it then you don't approve of the deal?"

"No, I don't. If I had been asked before it was made, I would've advised against it. The Chinese cannot be trusted. Not at all. We could transfer our arsenal to them, relying on their money and their protection, and as soon as they have enough weapons to fulfill their needs, which in my opinion is far fewer than what we're ultimately offering, they could terminate the agreement and there would be absolutely nothing we could do about it, and then we'd be left defenseless with our treasury quickly running dry.

"This entire deal is predicated upon the belief that because it lasts for thirty years, any sanctions currently imposed or to be imposed in reaction to the deal would've long been lifted. But that could take ten years, maybe twenty. And that assumes the president's ambitions end at the Ukrainian border, and you and I both know they don't. If the Chinese feel in three years or five years that they've got enough warheads to deter any American threats, and cut us off, our country is truly screwed, as the Americans might say, because not only will we be suffering under their sanctions, we'll have lost China as a trading partner and a source of lease payments. We'll be entirely isolated."

Peskov frowned, pursing his lips. All of the discussions surrounding the treaty had been conducted between him, the president, and three others. No one else. And none of them were military strategists. A mind that thought the way Nikitin's did should have been at the table to point out these shortcomings in their thinking. But it was too late for that now.

Nikitin rose. "One more thing. You might be interested to know that we figured out how Victor made contact with the Americans."

Peskov leaned back, his eyebrows climbing his forehead. "How?"

"At a bar that American embassy workers are known to frequent. We caught him on camera handing an envelope to a young woman we've identified as Gail Nichols. She was with another man from the embassy named Carl Garneau."

"Well, at least that explains that. When this is over, have their credentials yanked."

Nikitin headed for the door. "There's no point. They left yesterday. Their flight has probably already landed in the United States."

"Well, it might be worthwhile formally revoking their credentials just so they know we know how it happened."

"Very well."

Nikitin left and Peskov stared at the clock on the wall, his mind racing as he replayed the conversation that had just taken place. Could they have misread things? Could this actually be a bad deal? Could the Chinese eagerness to proceed be because it was mutually beneficial, or because they fully intended to renege on the deal once they had what they wanted? There was only one thing he was certain of.

Nikitin was right.

The Chinese could not be trusted.

Operations Center 3, CIA Headquarters
Langley, Virginia

Leroux rose as Morrison entered the operations center. He held up a classified folder. "Can I have everyone's attention?" The room quieted as the Chief joined Leroux at his workstation. "I assume you've all been briefed on the message the president sent both the Russian and Chinese earlier today."

Heads bobbed around the room, Leroux confirming. "I briefed them earlier, sir."

"Good. Well, we haven't had a response yet from the Russians, but we just received a response from the Chinese. The president agreed that since this team is running point on the operation, you should be filled in. Of course, repeat this to anyone and you'll be shot, yada, yada, yada. You won't be receiving a copy of this, but I'll give you the highlights. Basically, the Chinese are denying any knowledge of any agreement and are claiming that the document Victor provided us is a fake. They take great affront, blah, blah, blah. The usual nonsense."

Leroux grunted. "So, basically what we expected."

"Exactly, which suggests to me and the White House brain trust that they know damn well they've been caught with their pants down, but don't care, because they're more interested in getting their hands on those weapons."

"So, what do we do now?"

"The president is considering making a deal."

"Oh? What kind of deal?"

"If the Russians halt the weapons shipment and cancel the Chinese arms sale agreement, he'll agree to lift the cap on Russian oil and gas prices, and partially lift the ban on sales for humanitarian purposes. Sort of like what we had with the Iranians."

Packman cursed. "Then they still win in the end."

"Depends on how you look at it, I guess," replied Morrison. "The sanctions were always going to come off at some point. If we ease them off now and prevent the weapons sale, they're still going to lose in Ukraine. And if we stop the transfer of their nuclear arsenal to China, we maintain the balance of power. I'd rather let a slowly starving bear have that arsenal rather than a well-fed dragon. Remember, the goal here is to prevent the transfer of a massive nuclear arsenal to an enemy on the rise. If we can stop that by loosening the noose around our weaker enemy's throat slightly, we can deal with those consequences later. When's that first train due to arrive?"

"Six hours," replied Tong, checking her screen.

"Well, that's how many hours we have to deal with this. Otherwise, it's too late."

"Is the president going to allow that first train to cross the border?"

"He hasn't decided yet. Calling in an airstrike on Russian soil just might give the hawks in Russia the fuel they need to bring tactical nukes into the war and escalate this conflict far wider than it already is, though I don't see any alternative."

Leroux cleared his throat and Morrison regarded him.

"What is it?"

Leroux pointed at a map on the upper right corner of the display, a red dot flashing in Mongolia.

"What's that?"

"That could be the solution to our problem."

Genghis Khan International Airport
Ulan Bator, Mongolia

Kane grabbed his backpack off the luggage carousel and handed it to Sherrie before snatching hers. Their cover was newlyweds hiking around the world. It was a carefully crafted cover by Moscow Station that just needed faces on the IDs, so when he had called Chief of Station Arbuckle, she had been able to provide them with everything they needed within an hour, and they were on a flight two hours after that. They cleared customs, playing the madly-in-love couple for the bored official who asked the standard questions.

Kane always enjoyed working with Sherrie because she was easy to play the romantic parts with, and because the four of them were such good friends. Nothing ever got out of hand and nothing was ever misinterpreted, though if he were Leroux watching on a tapped security feed, he would probably be squirming with the fistful of ass Kane now gripped.

Their passports and visas were handed back, the hack on the Mongolian system confirming to the border agent that the forged paperwork was valid, and a young boy, perhaps 12 or 13, raced up to them.

"Do you need a taxi? My father's taxi, it's clean and cheap. He'll take you wherever you need to go."

"How cheap?" asked Kane.

"Cheaper than New York City."

"New York City's expensive. Cheaper than Moscow or Beijing?"

"Far cheaper."

Kane handed him his backpack, the code words exchanged. The boy insisted on taking Sherrie's as well, and they followed him out of the terminal and toward the taxi stand. Within minutes, they were driving into the city in what was indeed a clean and relatively modern vehicle for this poor country.

"Welcome to Ulan Bator," said their driver. "I'm Delger. You've met my son, Khasar." He jerked his thumb over his shoulder. "There's a care package in the back from Langley. Luckily our weapons cache here has everything that was on your list, but we're going to have a hell of a time getting you into position in time. We obviously can't do it by land. You'll never get there, and besides, there are too many random checkpoints, some legitimate, some not so much."

"I was thinking the same thing," said Kane. "We need to go by air."

Sherrie eyed him. "How the hell are we going to manage that?"

Delger grinned in the rearview mirror at them. "Don't you worry, I have a friend with a very good airplane, and he asks no questions, but I have to warn you."

"What's that?" asked Sherrie warily.

"His plane, not so clean."

Gorky Park
Moscow, Russia

Peskov sat on the park bench, his stomach churning at what he was doing. He had been enraged when he had discovered what Victor had done, betraying his country, yet here he sat, about to do the same thing, the same debate raging within that Victor must have had. The Chinese, as expected, had responded to the Americans with nothing but denials, but they had also responded to the Kremlin, indicating they wanted the deal to continue now that the leak had been plugged. Despite Washington's threats, the president was convinced it was the best course of action and had ordered everything to proceed regardless of what might come out of Washington or the UN meeting scheduled for later in the day.

It was, as predicted, talk and more talk, but there had also been listening, and it was he who had listened to Nikitin's warning. The Chinese couldn't be trusted. The more he thought about it, the more he was convinced that the long-term play by the Chinese was to betray them—secure the arsenal then cut off the payments.

He had brought up the possibility with the president, but the man refused to listen. He was convinced that this was the only course of action and insisted on proceeding. Once the man got an idea in his head, it was almost impossible to turn the ship. Unless he saw evidence of Chinese betrayal, he was hell-bent on continuing on this course that Peskov was almost certain would ultimately lead to their ruin.

So a call had been made, a call that now made him a traitor to his country, no better than Victor, though perhaps no worse. They had both come to the same conclusion and acted as patriots attempting to save their country rather than destroy it.

A woman sat on the bench beside him. He didn't look over. He knew who she was, Moscow Chief of Station Patricia Arbuckle.

"I was surprised to hear from you."

"No more surprised than I was to be calling you, I assure you."

"I assume this has to do with our little situation."

"It does."

"Does your president wish to communicate something confidentially?"

"Unfortunately, no. He's committed to his current course of action."

"Then what's the purpose of this meeting?"

"If we're to stop this, then I need a favor."

En Route to Russian Border, Mongolia

Kane sat in the copilot's seat of the 1960s-era Cessna Skyhawk, something that at best could now be described as a crop-duster, the beast having seen far better days. Delger's warning that the plane wasn't clean was inaccurate, unless you considered rust and rot dirt. Kane would have preferred filth, as he wasn't certain this bucket of rusting bolts could get them where they needed to go without first losing a wing.

Sherrie tapped him on the shoulder from the rear seat and pointed at the aileron. Kane's eyes bulged. "Is that duct tape?"

Their pilot, Jargal, leaned over to look at where Kane was pointing, then laughed. "No, that would be foolish. It's Gorilla tape. I ordered it off the Internet. Very strong."

Kane slapped his forehead, gripping his temples as he said a silent prayer.

I promise, God, if you get us through this, I'll try not to kill anyone for the rest of the day.

The plane jerked up and to the right as it hit some turbulence and Jargal struggled with the yoke for a moment. Kane glanced up, God apparently not satisfied with his offer.

Two days?

The plane leveled out and Kane checked his phone, tracking their progress. They were making good time despite their less than direct route. Between Jargal and Langley, they had mapped a route that would avoid population centers and standard patrols, and Jargal was hugging the ground to keep below Mongolia's primitive radar. The challenge would be when they reached the Russian border. They were one hour away from what was probably the most dangerous part of the mission, and assuming they survived, they had less than one hour after that to get into final position and take care of business, should they receive the order.

The question that still raged was what to do if they didn't receive the order. He had already come to a decision, but Sherrie would wear this too. He twisted in his seat to face her. "I want to blow it."

She smirked. "That's usually my line."

He gave her a look and Jargal roared. "I like her."

Kane chuckled. "Yeah, well, don't get any ideas. Her boyfriend can have you killed."

Jargal grinned. "It would be worth it."

"You know it would," said Sherrie, deadpan. "You want to blow the rail line. I take it you mean even if we don't get the order?"

"Exactly."

"What if the order is not to?"

"Is there a difference?"

"Yes, I think there is. One is taking the initiative and doing something that you believe is right. The other is disobeying an order that you believe is wrong."

He pursed his lips. His thinking had been predicated upon nobody making a decision one way or the other, leaving it up to him to take action. If he was ordered not to, Sherrie was right, that was a whole other ballgame. The problem here was the stakes were too high for indecision. It was why he had decided to take action himself. But if he was ordered not to, he would have to assume Washington had good reason other than cowardice.

Yet he still believed those weapons shouldn't be allowed to cross into Chinese territory.

"What do you think?" he asked.

Sherrie ran her fingers through her hair, tugging on the long golden locks. "I say if we don't hear anything, we blow it. But if they say no, then we have to obey the order, even if we see the train coming with the weapons. I don't see that we have a choice, do we? If Washington orders us to stand down, they must have their reasons."

She was right, though he disagreed. He sighed. "Fine. If we're ordered not to blow the tracks, then we won't."

Presidential Executive Office, The Kremlin
Moscow, Russia

Peskov read the translation of the Chinese intercept, suppressing the urge to smile as Nikitin sat staring at him.

"What do you make of it?" asked the FSB director.

"It would seem you were right. The Chinese do intend to betray us."

Nikitin smirked. "I won't bother saying I told you so, but perhaps the next time ideas like this are floated about, you should have someone with my background consulted."

Peskov sighed, allowing Nikitin his moment. "You're right, of course, but for now I need to take this to the president. He needs to see what the Chinese have planned so we can put an end to this before it's too late."

"Do you think he'll be convinced by such an obvious forgery?"

Peskov's eyes shot wide and his stomach flipped. "Excuse me?"

"Amateurs shouldn't be involved in the spy game."

Peskov shifted uncomfortably. "What do you mean?"

"I mean, everyone involved is being observed. Earlier today you met with Chief of Station Arbuckle from the American Embassy. You had a brief conversation without once making eye contact."

Peskov's shoulders slumped. "Would you believe it was a coincidence?"

Nikitin chuckled. "No. Though I'm impressed with the balls it displays. I was wondering what your game was until we intercepted this communique accidentally broadcasted on a Chinese frequency using an encryption protocol that we broke two months ago."

Peskov gripped the arms of his chair. "What are you going to do?"

"I'm going to help my country by helping you."

"How?"

"All evidence that you met with Arbuckle has already been wiped. The agents monitoring you were part of my personal investigations unit and have been sworn to secrecy. The intercept came through valid channels. The Americans did an excellent job in making it look like it came from the Chinese, and the protocols used and the wording all appear genuine. If I'm asked, I'll indicate there's no evidence that the message is a forgery, since there is indeed no evidence it is."

"How will you explain the encryption?"

"That it was transmitted from an office unaccustomed to sending such messages due to the highly compartmentalized nature of the document. Innocent human error."

"Do you think anyone would believe that?"

226

"The only person we need to convince is the president. If he believes you, then I doubt any questions will be asked."

"And if you're wrong?"

"Then tell him it can be looked into further, but that I'm confident it's genuine, and probing it further risks exposure. That should hopefully be enough to end this foolish escapade."

Peskov checked the clock and cursed. The first train would reach the border in less than an hour. He rose. "I better meet with him immediately, there's not much time left."

South of Dauriya, Russia

Kane peered at the ground below, lit only by the stars and a half moon. Lights flickered to the north from Dauriya, one of the last stops in Russia on the Trans-Siberian line before it crossed into China. They had bailed at 2000 feet just as they crossed the border, a low-altitude jump that had them coming in fast. It would be a hard landing, especially if they couldn't see the ground coming, which was why he was paying particular attention to Leroux's voice in his ear, reading off his altitude based upon a sensor in his watch.

His chute fluttered above him louder than it should at this altitude, and it was disconcerting. They had two shots at this—either he or Sherrie had to come out of this jump not only alive, but completely mobile. The last update from Langley just before they jumped had the Russian trains still rolling. Apparently, there was a Hail Mary underway that they couldn't share due to the highly classified nature of it. If it didn't work, they were a go for blowing the line, but he hoped it did, because blowing this line, even for good reason, wouldn't go over well.

"Two hundred feet," reported Leroux in his ear and he readied himself, relaxing every muscle in his body and bending his legs at the knees and hips.

"One hundred feet."

He pulled down on the toggles, flaring his chute.

"Fifty feet."

He could see the ground and it looked clear. He hit, and it was hard, but he immediately rolled, absorbing the impact then spinning onto his knees, hauling in his chute as Sherrie touched down nearby with a yelp.

"Control, Wild One, I'm on the ground and in one piece, over." He policed his chute, stuffing it back in its bag, then hurried over to Sherrie, still lying on the ground. He took a knee beside her. "You okay?"

She winced, gripping her ankle. "I rolled it. I don't think it's broken, but it's sprained. Bad."

He cursed. This was not what they needed right now. He grabbed the lines of her chute and hauled it in as she shrugged out of the harness. He stuffed her chute back in its bag then opened the supplies strapped to his chest and removed a med kit.

"We're going to have to wrap your ankle."

She dismissed the idea. "There's no time." She jerked her chin toward the tree line. "Just get me in those trees and you go take care of business. I'll follow if I can. Don't worry about me. Stopping that train is more important."

He sighed heavily. She was right, and if she weren't a good friend, he wouldn't even be hesitating in leaving her behind. "Okay, let's get you up." He hauled her to her feet and grabbed the two chutes and supply bags.

She held out her hand. "Give me some of that. It's just my ankle."

He handed her the chutes, slung one of the supply bags, and carried the other as she draped her arm over his shoulders. He helped her to the tree line, activating his comms. "Control, Wild One. Skylark is down with a possible sprained ankle, over."

The concern in Leroux's voice was obvious, though he remained professional. "Copy that, Wild One. What are your intentions, over?"

He reached the tree line and helped her sit against the trunk of a large tree. He quickly yanked out her chute, folding it into several layers and laying it on the ground. He helped her on it to keep her dry from the snow, then took the other chute, folding it again and covering her with it as she resorted their supply bags. "Control, I'll be proceeding with the mission solo, then when done, I'll retrieve her and head for the extraction point."

"Copy that, Wild One."

"ETA on that train?"

"You've got twenty minutes to get into position."

"Copy that." He grabbed Sherrie's hand and squeezed it. "You good?"

"Don't worry about me. I'm fine. Now get the hell out of here and stop that train."

He gave her a peck on the cheek. She patted one of the re-sorted bags beside her. "Everything you'll need when out for a nice hike in southeastern Russia."

He grinned. "It would've been one hell of a honeymoon." He grabbed the bag and rose, strapping it to his back. "I'll be back before you know it." He checked his phone's GPS, took a bearing, then set off at a jog—sprinting through a forest wouldn't be wise. They couldn't afford any more twisted ankles, not if he was going to be the world's last line of defense.

Operations Center 3, CIA Headquarters
Langley, Virginia

Leroux leaned back, muttering a curse. Sherrie was incapacitated in enemy territory in a region that would be swarming with troops the moment Kane set off the explosives. The only hope was to get her into Mongolia. She was only three miles from the border, but it might as well be thirty depending on how bad her ankle was.

He turned to Tong. "We need an LZ near the border, Mongolian side."

Tong shook her head. "The region's pretty rocky."

"Then contact the pilot, see if he knows of something."

"I'm on it."

He faced Packman. "What's the status of those trains?"

"They're all still rolling. No evidence that whatever Washington's trying is working."

Leroux cursed. He had been briefed by Morrison on the Hail Mary initiated from someone on the Russian side of things. The fake Chinese communique was a long shot that had to work, otherwise either Kane would be forced to take action, or an impossible deal would be struck, a deal that could cost the lives of hundreds of thousands of people by prolonging an already brutal war.

South of Dauriya, Russia

Sherrie finished wrapping her ankle, wincing as she tied it off. She gently rotated it and gasped. There was no way she was putting pressure on that, not anytime soon. She popped a fistful of painkillers. Ibuprofen. Not the good stuff. She wouldn't be joining the fun. The job now was to save herself. While she would like to assume Kane would be successful and would return for her, she couldn't count on that. But even if he did, any distance she could cover herself would be time saved that they might desperately need. Right now, there was no indication the Russians knew they were here, otherwise Langley would have reported it.

She needed to get mobile.

She surveyed the immediate area and found what she needed, just out of reach. "Here goes nothing." She rolled several times, closing the distance between her and a broken branch lying on the ground. She grabbed it then rolled back, her ankle protesting the entire way. She retrieved a small hatchet out of the gear and began trimming the branch, fashioning a crutch that would hopefully allow her to get underway.

But even if it didn't, at least it made her feel useful.

Presidential Executive Office, The Kremlin
Moscow, Russia

Peskov stood in the president's office, his hands clasped behind his back as he struggled to remain calm. He had grown accustomed to his country's leader flying off the handle over the past year, what with the nearly constant bad news from the front, but this was an entirely different level of rage. The man had been screaming for almost half an hour and was becoming hoarse. Peskov had said almost nothing since he had relayed the details of the fake communique, and there was no doubt from the man's reaction that he believed it to be genuine.

He finally stopped, draining a glass of water on his desk, his beet-red face slowly returning to normal before he sat. "It's time for a reply to the Americans."

Peskov forced himself to remain composed, hiding the surprise. "What do you plan to say to them?"

"I plan to tell them to go to hell!"

Southeast of Dauriya, Russia

Kane peered through his binoculars at the tracks below, cut through the countryside. He scanned up and down the Trans-Siberian line, finding no evidence of patrols. He was just three miles from the Chinese border to the south of him, but the railway had another thirty miles before it turned south to cross into China where the bulk of the security was located for both sides. For now, it appeared he was clear.

He activated his comms. "Control, Wild One. I'm in position, over."

"Copy that, Wild One. We're showing a patrol on a utility road west of your position, two klicks out, heading in your direction. No evidence it's anything but routine, over."

"Copy that. ETA my location?"

"Five minutes."

Kane cursed. He needed ten to reach the tracks, plant the explosives, then return to cover. "Copy that, Control. What's the ETA on that train?"

"Twenty minutes."

"It's going to be close," he muttered. "Copy that, Control. I'm going to hold position until the patrol passes. What's the status on Skylark?"

"Skylark is heading for the extraction point."

Kane cocked an eyebrow. "Oh? Is her ankle better?"

"Negative, Wild One, she's apparently fashioned herself a crutch."

He cursed. If she ran into a patrol, there was no way she could outrun them. She should have stayed put. She was doing it for him. Any distance she could shave off before he reached her meant less time they would both be slowed by her injury. He likely would have done the same, though it didn't make it the right decision, but he wasn't about to second guess a fellow officer over live comms. "Understood, Control. Try to keep her out of sight. Once these explosives go off, the Russians are going to send everything they've got into the area."

"Roger that, Wild One. We're keeping her along the tree lines. That patrol's about to reach your position."

Kane peered through his binoculars at the utility road that ran alongside the tracks, a light armored vehicle, its headlights bouncing along a road that had seen better days, now in sight. "Wild One going silent. Out." He hunkered down and lowered his binoculars just in case a stray beam of light caused a reflection, and waited, worried more about Sherrie than himself.

Director Morrison's Office, CIA Headquarters
Langley, Virginia

Leroux entered Morrison's office, gasping for breath, having run the entire way. Morrison pointed at a chair and Leroux dropped into it, his chest heaving. "I've got to do more cardio."

"Apparently," agreed Morrison. He tapped his screen. "We just received a reply from the Russians to our initial communique."

Leroux glanced at his phone to see if there were any new updates from Tong and found nothing. "As far as I know, sir, the trains are still rolling."

"They are."

"What was the response?"

"Surprisingly frank, with I think genuine elements of truth to it. White House analysts believe it was prepared in a hurry, and I think we both know why."

"The fake communique. They're buying it."

222222222222

2 stop

"Exactly, and they know that train with the first delivery is about to cross, so they're trying to get last-minute concessions out of us."

"What do they want?"

"They want all restrictions on their oil and natural gas exports lifted."

Leroux frowned. "So, pretty much what the president was thinking of offering them regardless."

"Yes."

"What's the president going to do?"

"A decision hasn't been made, though I have made a recommendation."

"And what's that?"

"Call their bluff. They're in a panic because they believe the Chinese are going to screw them, so there's no way they're going to let those weapons cross the border. I recommended letting them hang. Force their hand. They'll have to stop the trains themselves."

"And if they don't, if they decide to let the first shipment go?"

"Then Kane's in position to stop them." Morrison paused. "He is, right?"

Leroux nodded. "Just before I left he was waiting for a patrol to pass, then he needs ten minutes. It's going to be tight, but unless something goes wrong, he should be able to take out the tracks in time. Do you think the president's going to follow your advice?"

Morrison shrugged. "I have no idea. It depends on who's got his ear today. He'll listen to his own people before he listens to me, and there were a lot of scared people on that teleconference. I know there are people urging him to make the deal, but there were a few others saying the same thing I am."

"What are Kane's orders if a decision isn't made in time?"

"Unless I hear different, his orders stand. Stop that train."

Southeast of Dauriya, Russia

Kane sprinted down the slope toward the tracks just as the patrol drove out of sight. He skidded to a halt on the gravel then dropped to his knees. He shrugged out of his backpack and unzipped it, pulling out the C4 provided by their Mongolian contact, Delger. He scooped out some gravel and placed the charge, then inserted the detonator and activated the device. He pushed the gravel back to hide it from prying eyes just in case an unexpected patrol returned, then repeated the process on the second track.

He took a brief moment to inspect his handiwork when a train whistled in the distance coming from the town just up the line. It had to be the weapons train—no other train was scheduled for another hour. He scrambled back up the slope and hit the deck. He peered through his binoculars at his handiwork and cursed. The disturbed gravel was a distinctly different color than the surrounding stone, something he hadn't been able to see when he was too close to the problem. It was likely because the bottom of some of the gravel was wet and, when disturbed, the wet darker side got turned up.

There was nothing he could do about it now.

He activated his comms. "Control, Wild One. Explosives planted. ETA on that train?"

"It's just left Dauriya. ETA your position four minutes, over," reported Tong.

"Copy that, Control. Am I a go or no go for detonation?"

A breathless Leroux cut in, replacing Tong. "Wild One, this is Control Actual. You're to stand by. I repeat, stand by, over."

Kane cursed. "Control, Washington does realize that it takes time for a train to stop, don't they? If I don't detonate now, that thing could derail."

"Understood, Wild One. Our new orders are to hold off on authorization. Be advised, your patrol is returning. ETA two minutes."

Kane growled. The timing on this was terrible. "Control, am I being ordered to not detonate, or do I still have operational discretion?"

There was a pause, and it was clear Leroux was formulating his words carefully. "My orders are to not give you the go until ordered to do so."

"So, my standing orders have not changed?"

"Affirmative."

"That's all I needed to hear. Wild One, out."

Sherrie leaned against a tree, her ankle throbbing. She would be surprised if she had covered half a mile since she started, but she had to keep going. She had no choice. She was tempted to stuff snow into her sock to act as an ice pack, but it would just melt and eventually freeze her foot, then she could be dealing with frostbite and permanent damage. She wasn't going to lose her operational status over a sprained ankle.

Langley had requested she stay off comms unless it was absolutely necessary as they dealt with the ongoing operation. She was desperate to know what was going on, though she understood the restriction. She had expected the explosives to have detonated at least five minutes ago, and so far she had heard nothing. Something was obviously going on, something that had either delayed Kane, or he had been ordered not to proceed.

A train whistle in the distance hinted at the necessity of the mission proceeding. It had to be the train they were here to stop, and it was close and on schedule. She pushed off the tree she had been leaning against and resumed her slow trek, each step torture.

And one step closer to freedom.

Presidential Executive Office, The Kremlin
Moscow, Russia

Peskov stared at the terminal, a direct link between Washington and Moscow. He wasn't sure what he was expecting. The reply had been delivered not even half an hour ago. If the president hadn't ranted for almost an hour, there might have been enough time for the Americans to actually respond, but there wasn't, unless they were willing to be as hasty in their answer as his side had just been. The president was calling their bluff, sending the train to the border, daring the Americans to respond either militarily, diplomatically, or not at all, risking the weapon systems making it into Chinese hands.

The suspense was nearly killing him.

Nikitin entered the room. "Anything?"

"No."

Nikitin checked his watch. "That train reaches the border in less than ten minutes. Is there any indication of what the president's going to do?"

"No. I fear this might be a matter of pride with him," he said, lowering his voice. "Once he sets out on a path…" He trailed off, not needing to complete his sentence. "I think he's going to let the train pass, take the money, then use the other trains as leverage to get the Americans to play ball."

Nikitin's head bobbed. "It's a good strategy, one that even I might employ at this point."

"I thought you were against the deal."

"I am. I never would have allowed us to get to this point. But now that we're here, we need to make the best of a bad situation. If the Americans are willing to deal but won't do so without a little incentive, then allowing six missile systems to cross the border might just be the impetus they need to meet at least some of our demands. Half a dozen of these things doesn't change the balance of power by being in Chinese hands, but it just might maintain the balance by leaving ours."

Peskov chewed his cheek as he considered Nikitin's words. The man was right. If they stopped the trains, it meant the Americans would know the deal with the Chinese was off and there would be no incentive for them to capitulate. But allowing that first train across the border, that could be just enough to get them to play ball. He glanced toward the president's office with an appreciative smile. "He's a master strategist."

Nikitin agreed. "He started playing this game long before anyone ever heard of him."

Southeast of Dauriya, Russia

Kane cursed as his worst fears came true. The patrol had spotted his handiwork and stopped to investigate. Four soldiers were heading from the utility road to the tracks. They would discover the explosives any moment now. The question was, were any of them trained to deactivate them? And even if they weren't, detonating them now meant killing four Russian soldiers rather than merely damaging tracks that could be replaced within a day.

He could see the light from the train approaching, the chug of its engine echoing across the landscape as it continued to gain speed. A decision had to be made.

"Control, Wild One. Any word, over?"

"Negative, Wild One."

"Understood. Exercising operational independence." He drew his weapon and fired four rounds, taking out the rear tire of the light armored vehicle. The soldiers scattered, one of them pointing in his direction, obviously with the presence of mind to have taken note as to where the shots had come from.

Kane remained at a crouch as they regrouped and spread out, heading in his direction, one of them on a radio. He readied the detonator, waiting for his enemy to get far enough away that they wouldn't be blown apart. "Come on, come on!" He could see the train now, and it was too damn close. Whatever warning the troops had called in hadn't reached the engineer, yet there was one warning he could give that wouldn't be missed.

All four cleared the utility road and he triggered the explosives. A deafening roar overwhelmed the train's engine, a brilliant flash lighting the entire area. He opened his eyes and peered through the binoculars to confirm the tracks were a twisted wreck, and all four Russians were down but still alive. He pushed to his feet, sprinting away from the scene as shouts erupted behind him and the train's brakes squealed.

His comms squawked. "Wild One, Control Actual. You'll be happy to know we just received the orders to take out the tracks."

Kane smiled. "Understood. In the final report, let's work on that timeline, shall we?"

"Roger that, Wild One. We'll make it look like it was their idea."

Sherrie spun toward the twin explosions. The night sky behind her briefly lit and brakes squealed as the rumble settled, but she ignored it as she pressed on with renewed urgency. This area would be filthy with Russians shortly, and the more distance she put between herself and the scene of the crime, the better. Unfortunately, she was a sitting duck.

She had two miles to cover to get to the border, and as soon as the Russians got helicopters in here with infrared gear, they would spot her in a heartbeat and it would be over.

Her comms squawked in her ear and her heart ached at the love of her life's voice, a voice she might never hear in person again. "Skylark, Control. Mission update. The tracks have been taken out. Wild One is heading for your position. Unfortunately, he had to engage four hostiles, so they're aware he's here and what direction he's heading. What's your status, over?"

"Control, Skylark, acknowledged. Current status is ankle is still screwed up. I'm making best speed toward the extraction point, however, there's no way in hell I can make the border."

"Understood, Skylark. Continue at best possible speed. We'll keep you posted on enemy activity."

"Copy that, Control. Skylark, out." She pressed forward, grimacing through the pain, debating what to do. They were pursuing Kane, but he might reach her before he was captured. If he did, she would slow him down, and they would both end up in the hands of an angry enemy. She could think of only one solution. Unfortunately, it was one her friend would never agree to.

He had to leave her behind, save himself, and leave her to be captured as the saboteur.

It was the only way they both wouldn't die here tonight.

Kane sprinted along the tree line. He couldn't hear his pursuers over the squealing of brakes, the train continuing its far too-slow deceleration. He reached a ridgeline and looked back, cursing at the first of two locomotives derailed as it reached the sabotaged tracks. The incredibly heavy machine inexorably continued forward, the inertia built during its run-up from its last stop dooming those aboard. The locomotive tipped on its side, slamming into the ground, the impact so powerful, he felt the vibration.

The train continued to slide forward off the rails, the second locomotive following the first, before the first car containing one of the terrifying nuclear weapons systems teetered then tipped. He winced then gasped as it hit the ground, the container slipping off the car and careening into the dead weight of the second locomotive. The container folded like a tin can, then a massive explosion erupted. He spun around, shielding his eyes as he threw himself to the ground. The entire area shook and a surge of warm air raced past him. He pushed up from the snow and looked back when another detonation flashed. He covered his eyes once again as car after car exploded, lighting the night as if it were day.

Anybody on that train was dead, including, to his dismay, a railcar bringing up the rear, loaded with troops guarding the cargo. Thankfully, he heard no cries, no screams. They had been killed instantly. He turned over, propped up on his elbows, and stared at the horror he had created. It was why he had pushed and pushed for permission to detonate the train with enough time to stop, but never in his wildest dreams would he have thought the Russians would be foolish enough to actually transport the weapon systems with the rockets fully fueled. If their tanks had been drained like they should have been, the train would have still derailed, but there wouldn't have been any explosion, no fire. Those aboard would have survived with nothing more than broken bones and bruises.

But now scores were dead, and he just prayed that the warheads' safety systems had done their job and prevented any spread of radioactive material. He wasn't worried about a detonation. That's not how nuclear weapons worked, but contamination was a possibility, and he had to limit his exposure. He rose and resumed his escape. There was no way he could let himself be captured, not after this.

The Russians would be out for blood.

Operations Center 3, CIA Headquarters
Langley, Virginia

Leroux shot to his feet, his jaw dropping as the satellite footage repeatedly flashed, massive explosions erupting upward and out as the worst-case scenario played out. He pointed at Tong. "Please tell me that's not nuclear."

She checked her readings. "Negative. It's too small and the satellite's not detecting any residual indicators." She faced him. "Those idiots transported the rockets fully fueled."

He closed his eyes as he sank back into his chair. "Unbelievable." What should have been a simple act of sabotage that halted the train for a day or two while the tracks were repaired and giving the diplomats time to do their work, had turned into a disaster. Not only was over a hundred million dollars of Russian military hardware destroyed, but scores of its soldiers guarding the cargo were dead, and the lone direct rail route between China and Russia was completely destroyed for at least half a mile. From what he could see on the screen, the craters left behind had blown away the track bed, meaning it could take weeks to repair the vital trade corridor.

He activated his comms. "Wild One, Control, come in, over."

"This is Wild One. Go ahead."

He sighed with relief at his friend's voice. "Wild One, what's your status?"

"A little singed, but I'm all right. I'm trying to put as much distance as I can between me and that Charlie Foxtrot. Any indication of radiation?"

"Not at this end. Check your phone. It has a built-in detector."

Kane cursed, apparently having forgotten this fact. "Stand by." A moment later he replied. "Looks like we're good for now. I'm not seeing anything but background radiation. Hopefully, those fires will burn themselves out sooner rather than later. Otherwise, things might change."

Leroux stared at the still raging aftermath, each weapon containing enough rocket fuel to propel its missile high enough to rain death upon a target almost 7000 miles away.

Packman's keyboard clicked behind him, and a moment later another angle from the satellite appeared.

"We've got activity in Zabaikal'sk. Looks like Russian Army and first responders heading onto the utility road."

"ETA?"

"About twenty to thirty minutes."

"Copy that. Keep me posted on aerial activity."

"Yes, sir."

"And Sonya, any word from our friend yet?"

She frowned. "No, I haven't been able to raise him. His satphone keeps ringing then goes to voicemail. Either something's happened to him, or he's away from his phone."

Leroux cursed. "Keep trying. He might be the only way to save our people."

Presidential Executive Office, The Kremlin
Moscow, Russia

The army's Kremlin liaison rushed into Peskov's office, his eyes wide. "Sir, we have reports of a massive explosion on the Trans-Siberian Railway!"

Peskov shot to his feet. "What?"

"Just short of the border, about thirty kilometers." He shook a piece of paper. "The reports are sketchy, but it looks like a patrol found something on the tracks, radioed it in, and then moments later there was an explosion. The train engineer reported it, but we lost all contact. A couple of minutes later, our people in Zabaikal'sk reported massive fireballs in the distance." The man's arms collapsed to his sides. "Who could have done this? Ukrainian terrorists?"

Peskov held out his hand and the colonel passed him the report. "You're dismissed. Keep me posted. I want whoever did this found. Alive."

"Yes, sir."

The colonel left the office and Nikitin, sitting quietly the entire time, reached over and closed the door. "I'm impressed that the Americans had the courage to actually act."

Peskov slumped in his chair. "I'm stunned. But why would they destroy it? Why not disable the tracks?"

"That's likely what they were attempting to do. But even if that train derailed, what the colonel just reported shouldn't have happened."

Peskov's eyes narrowed. "What do you mean?"

"I mean, why the hell weren't the tanks on those rockets drained before transport? If they hadn't been full, we'd merely be cleaning up the mess of a derailment. But now six of our most advanced weapons systems are destroyed, we have a potential radiological problem, and we look like fools to the Chinese."

Peskov rose. "I have to inform the president."

"What are you going to tell him?"

"I'm going to recommend that all the trains return to base to confirm the fuel status of the rockets, and that we abandon the plan, since not only do we have the intercept indicating the Chinese intent to renege on the deal, but that it's simply too dangerous to attempt such a rapid transfer of such dangerous weaponry."

Nikitin regarded him. "And what do you think he'll say?"

"He's a wise man. Hopefully, he'll agree that we must put an end to this, otherwise, something far worse could happen, something we can't cover up."

South of Dauriya, Russia

Kane pushed forward, passing where he had left Sherrie less than an hour ago. He couldn't hear any pursuers at the moment, but Langley had just reported choppers were inbound and the search would begin in earnest when they arrived. Sherrie was less than a mile ahead, having covered a good chunk of distance on her injured ankle. He could keep ahead of anybody pursuing him on foot, but as soon as Sherrie entered the equation, they would be covering half as much ground as those following them.

The question was what to do? There was no way to save both of them. As far as he was concerned, there was no doubt whom he was choosing to survive—his best friend's girlfriend, his friend, his fellow officer, whom he had no doubt had already come to the opposite conclusion. When he reached her, she would tell him to go on without her, and she would remain behind to be captured as the saboteur. It was the best way for one of the two of them to survive, for he could reach the border with ease if he didn't have to help her.

But surviving wasn't everything. Being able to live with oneself was sometimes more. If he left her behind to be tortured to death, he could never look at himself in the mirror again. He could never look his best friend in the eye. His life would effectively be over regardless.

He continued forward, staring at the map on his phone, and an idea occurred to him, an idea that might just save them both.

Operations Center 3, CIA Headquarters
Langley, Virginia

"Uh-oh," said Packman, the concern in his voice having Leroux turning in his chair.

"What?"

"Kane's changed direction. He's heading due south."

"South? He should be heading southwest."

"I know, but he's definitely heading south."

"Does he see something we don't?" Leroux turned back to examine the satellite images, the computer tracking all movement of enemy forces. Search parties had deployed from the utility road in all directions, with the vast majority of the resources headed southwest, in the direction they already knew Kane had headed. Dogs had arrived fifteen minutes ago, and the first helicopters would be in the area within another ten. If they were equipped with infrared sensors, the pursuit would be over fairly quickly.

Tong looked at him. "Could he be trying to lead them away from Sherrie?"

Leroux bit his lip. It was exactly the type of thing Kane would do—sacrifice himself to save someone else. His eyes shot wide as an idea occurred to him. "Wait a minute, bring up a map of the area. Show his position."

Tong complied.

"Zoom out, just a bit."

The image updated and he pointed. "Look, he's two klicks from the Chinese border, four clicks from the Mongolian. He's going to lead them away from Sherrie, hopefully giving her time to make her extraction. All he needs to do is get into China. The Russians can't pursue him. Then if he can evade the Chinese, he could scoot along their border to Mongolia and back in."

Child spun in his chair. "Sounds easy-peasy."

Leroux grunted at the sarcasm. "Yeah, but it's the only way both of them might be saved."

"Won't the dogs pick up her scent anyway?"

Tong groaned as she pointed at the screen. "Not if he keeps doing that."

The satellite zoomed in on Kane, showing him painting the snow and waving up at the sky.

"Looks like a K."

Child tapped at his keyboard. An isolated image appeared showing what Kane had written in the snow with a healthy stream of urine, confirming Tong's suspicions. It was a K. "That should keep the dogs distracted."

Presidential Executive Office, The Kremlin

Moscow, Russia

Peskov hung up his phone, his eyes burning with fatigue, his shoulders aching, and his throat still throbbing from where he had been punched. He was utterly exhausted, but it was over, the last of the calls made ordering the trains to be sent back to their bases, the weapons to be unloaded and returned to regular deployment. The side deal was off, the Americans having proven their resolve, and the president, once he had a chance to think, deciding that moving forward with a partner one knew was going to betray you wasn't wise, despite any short-term gains.

They were still attempting to salvage the conventional weapons deal, but the Americans had threatened sanctions should even that proceed, and he had a sense the Chinese were going to walk away from everything if they lost the leverage a massive nuclear arsenal would have provided. There had been no official communication with the

Chinese yet. Everything was still happening too quickly, and it was knee-jerk reactions that kept getting them into trouble.

Nikitin entered, closing the door.

"Have they caught the saboteur yet?"

Nikitin sat. "No. The dogs have picked up the scent and it appears he's heading south to China."

Peskov cursed. "Didn't this take place only a few kilometers shy of the border?"

"Yes."

"Can we reach him in time?"

"We have a chopper inbound now that should be able to intercept him, but it'll be close. Once he crosses that border, there's nothing we can do."

"We can tell the Chinese. They could pick him up."

Nikitin eyed him. "If they pick him up, they'll interrogate him. Do you really want the Chinese to learn how incompetent we've been during this entire matter?"

Peskov sighed, gripping his temples. "Just for once I'd like something to go right."

"I think we should just be thankful if we get out of this one alive."

Peskov tensed at the comment, and sweat trickled down his back at the realization that someone still had to pay for what had happened. And with Victor having escaped and his father dead, the list of eligible candidates was growing shorter.

Russia/Chinese Border

Russia

Kane sprinted down the gentle slope as the chopper thundered behind him, rapidly approaching as he neared Chinese territory. They were in the middle of nowhere, so the border wasn't guarded, merely patrolled, a path cleared through the trees on the Chinese side marking the boundary with a road running along it. Once he reached that road, they couldn't pursue him, not without risking a Chinese response.

A light shone down on him and he skidded to a halt, spinning around and taking aim. He fired two shots, taking out the light, causing the pilot to jerk the stick from inexperience. Kane resumed his sprint and the chopper overtook him, hovering ahead just short of the border, and he cursed as four lines were tossed, troops following a moment later.

He had no choice.

It was him or them.

He stopped, aimed, and put two rounds in one of his enemy. The man cried out, falling to the ground as Kane put two more rounds in a second. An AK-74 opened up on him, and he dove to his left, rolling onto his back and firing up into the hold of the chopper, causing enough confusion for the gunner to cease fire. He rolled onto his stomach and took out a third of the soldiers inserting, but the fourth reached the ground, immediately pouring lead on Kane's position.

He rolled again, emptying the rest of his mag, then rapidly reloaded as his opponent scrambled for cover. The AK-74 opened up again from the chopper and Kane rose, sprinting forward, narrowing the angle between him and the gunner, forcing him to lean out to maintain fire. Kane raised his hand and fired a single shot, then returned his attention to his lone opponent on the ground, firing half a dozen more at him, several finding their mark. The man collapsed and Kane continued forward, emptying his weapon on the chopper overhead, forcing the pilot to bank away once again.

He was almost at the border now. The question was, would the Chinese be there to greet him?

Operations Center 3, CIA Headquarters
Langley, Virginia

Leroux jumped to his feet, fists pumping the air in triumph as the room erupted with cheers and applause, the Russian helicopter banking away, Kane emerging from under it still alive, still in one piece, racing toward the Chinese border less than half a mile away.

Child spun in his chair with a huge smile. "Like, my God, that guy's incredible! How the hell does he do it?"

Packman laughed. "Who cares, as long as he keeps doing it."

Tong beamed a smile at the group. "I hate to interrupt, but I thought you might like to know that all of the remaining trains are either holding position or reversing direction."

Leroux returned to his seat, his grin becoming painful. They had stopped it. They had won, and this entire ordeal was almost over. He spotted Marc Therrien in the back of the room out of the corner of his eye, raising a hand.

"Everyone quiet down!"

Leroux turned, his chest tightening at Therrien's grave expression. "What is it?"

Therrien pointed at the displays. "One of the dog teams picked up Sherrie's trail."

Leroux spun to see an isolated segment of the satellite footage showing a team of four with two dogs rapidly closing in on Sherrie's position, and as quickly as his heart had filled with hope and joy just a moment ago, it abandoned him.

South of Dauriya, Russia

Sherrie had no time to mourn the loss of her friend as she hobbled back into the trees, taking a position behind a large tree, using its massive trunk as shielding against the approaching enemy. She transferred her two spare mags into her left outer pocket so she could retrieve them quickly, then removed her gloves.

She had a decision to make. Tong had just reported four guards and two dogs. She didn't want to kill an animal, and she hoped it wouldn't come to that, but it might, and she had to prepare herself, because a moment of indecision could result in her being torn apart by the animals, trained no doubt by the Russians to be vicious. And with so many of their fellow soldiers dead in the explosion, these men would be out for revenge, unconcerned with orders to bring her in alive. If it looked like she would be eaten alive, she had to take the shot, no matter how much it broke her heart.

The barking was loud now, and she spotted the search party emerging from the trees, the dogs following her scent across the clearing. She waited for them to be completely in the open, then took aim.

Please God, forgive me.

She fired a single round into the left-most target, then adjusted her aim and squeezed the trigger again, rapidly repeating the process two more times. All four men dropped and the dogs pulled against their leashes still gripped in their dead masters' hands.

She breathed a sigh of relief at her momentary reprieve, and reached into her bag, removing some of the emergency rations—beef jerky, packed with enough protein to satisfy man or beast. She emerged from behind the tree with a smile, a gun in one hand, jerky in the other, and headed for the dogs in the hopes of a temporary truce.

Kane sprinted across the road hugging the Chinese border and dove into the ditch on the far side. The helicopter hovered in the distance, a second one rapidly inbound while flashlights bobbed on the ground as the search parties on foot closed in. But they weren't his concern anymore, and frankly, the more the merrier, for it meant they weren't after Sherrie. There was no way the Russians were going to cross the border and risk an incident with the Chinese.

He was safe from them now.

Gunfire rang out, four rapid shots, all from a Makarov, then silence. It had to be Sherrie, and the fact no one responded to the gunfire suggested she had gotten the drop on her own pursuers. He activated his comms. "Control, Wild One. I'm on the Chinese side of the border. I just heard some shots. What's the status on Skylark, over?"

Leroux responded. "You're not going to believe this, Wild One, but Skylark just took out the entire search team and is now feeding the dogs."

"Well, tell her to stop making nice and to get a move on." He peered through his binoculars. "It looks to me like some of the guys after me are redeploying in the direction of those shots. Her whole area's going to be swarming with troops in the next fifteen minutes."

"Relaying that now, Wild One."

"What's the status on the Chinese?"

"We're seeing activity at their border station to your east. They can probably hear all the gunfire, and they certainly would have heard those explosions. You've got three klicks to the Mongolian border and a clear road. I suggest you use it. We'll monitor for any activity and give plenty of warning."

"Copy that, Control. Wild One, out." Kane removed his backpack and every other piece of equipment he didn't need, keeping only his phone, pistol, and spare mags. He stashed everything in the trees, then stepped back out onto the road. He took a glance to the east where the Chinese were mobilizing, then turned west and ran as hard and as fast as he could with boots on a snow-covered road, all the while watching the Russian activity to his right, praying for a miracle to save Sherrie.

Sherrie was making better time now, as she had found a rhythm with her makeshift walking stick that had her barely putting pressure on her foot anymore, plus the fistful of painkillers she had taken had finally kicked in. She wasn't as fast as her healthy self, but at least she was moving at a decent clip. Unfortunately, the repetitive rhythm gave her time to think about her fallen comrade. Her boyfriend must be taking it hard, as she hadn't heard him on her comms since the helicopter had taken Kane out.

A helicopter, perhaps *the* helicopter, had just landed in the clearing where she had killed her four pursuers, and her comms chirped in her ear with an expected update from Tong. "Skylark, Control. We've got no evidence of pursuit from the chopper at this time, probably because they don't have anyone left alive but the crew, over."

Sherrie's eyes narrowed. "What do you mean?"

"It's the chopper that Kane engaged earlier. He took out at least five. It caused them to break off pursuit."

She froze. "Wait a minute. Dylan's alive?"

"Yes. Why? Were you told otherwise?"

She cried out in relief. "No, I just assumed. Who the hell can take on a helicopter?"

Tong laughed. "Well, I can name one person."

Sherrie tossed her head back and groaned in relief. "Thank God! I thought he was dead. What's his status?"

"He's on the Chinese side of the border on a utility road, giving Tom Cruise a run for his money."

"How far is he from the Mongolian border?"

"Less than three klicks, but don't you worry about him. He'll be fine. We need to worry about you. Once they've recovered from the setback you just gave them, they'll resume pursuit."

Sherrie had to agree with Tong's assessment. "I've still got almost two klicks. I'm making better time, but in my condition, there's no way I'm taking on a chopper." She continued forward. "Figure out a way for me out of this. I want to live long enough to give Kane a kick in the ass for making me worry so much."

Tong laughed. "Working on it."

Tsagaannuur, Mongolia

Jargal leaned back and patted his stomach as he chewed the last of the stew. He leaned over and gave Zolzaya a kiss, a widow he had met several years ago after flying her husband's body home from the capital city. Apparently, he was a bastard who beat her, so she had been incredibly grateful to the man who brought back his corpse so she could spit on it. They had immediately hit it off, and he flew up here regularly to visit. Today was just a quickie and some food because he had to head to the extraction point shortly.

He rose. "I have to go, otherwise I'm going to be late."

"Aw."

He laughed, giving her a hug, holding her tight. "You should move to the city. We'd see each other all the time."

She dismissed the idea. "This is my home. I can't leave."

He sighed, staring into her beautiful eyes. "Then maybe one day I'll have to move here."

She beamed a smile at him. "I like the sound of that."

He patted both her shoulders. "All right, I've got to go. I'll see you next time I'm through the area, hopefully in about a week."

She helped him into his jacket and he gave her one last passionate kiss before heading out the door of her yurt. He strode toward the rough landing strip used by the small village, and climbed into his pride and joy, firing up the engine. He grabbed the satellite phone off the copilot's seat. Forty-two missed calls, twelve messages.

Uh-oh.

Director Nikitin's Office, FSB Headquarters
Moscow, Russia

Nikitin sat in his office at FSB headquarters, exhausted. It had been a long two days, a very long two days, but it appeared the crisis had been averted, and he hoped the president's office now knew he should be consulted in the future on things of such importance. Yet it was something he would never suggest to the president. The man didn't take criticism well, and never tolerated failure.

Nothing good would come of the past couple of days. America and its allies would win diplomatically, and relations with China were immeasurably harmed with the cancelation of the deal. He just hoped they could salvage the conventional arms deal. He was, after all, a patriot and supported the war and his president, even when the man made a mistake.

He had learned long ago that when mistakes were made by powerful men, not only did you never point it out, you always provided a fall guy so the man could save face. Before he had left the Kremlin to return to

FSB headquarters, the Lubyanka building still undergoing repairs from the events of a couple of weeks ago, he had been called into the president's office and asked his opinion.

His answer was swift, unequivocal, and well-rehearsed. "Your plan was brilliant, Mr. President. There was no way anyone could have anticipated that the Chinese would betray us, nor that such incompetence would be displayed in the implementation."

Then a scapegoat had been named from a very short list, and it was too bad.

Because he actually liked the guy.

South of Dauriya, Russia

Sherrie checked her GPS. Still over one klick to go. She had made it farther than she had ever expected, but it wasn't going to be enough. The Russians had resumed their pursuit, dozens of troops closing in on her position from three sides, with dogs whose loyalty she had bought again on the hunt, their memories like goldfish.

Perhaps the soldiers they were with had better treats.

She didn't have enough ammo to take them all on, nor could she get the drop on so many. This was the end. She was exhausted, she was in pain, and it was time to die with dignity.

She activated her comms. "Control, this is Skylark requesting Control Actual, over." She picked a tree with a good view of the sun just starting to rise, and sat against it, extending out her wounded limb, sighing in relief.

"This is Control Actual," responded the love of her life. "What's your status?"

Tears rolled down her cheeks, not from self-pity, but for the pain the only man she had ever loved was about to experience. "Can you isolate our frequency?"

"Stand by." His voice cracked as if he knew what was coming. "We're isolated. What's wrong?"

She leaned her head back against the tree. "I can't go on. I've got nothing left in the tank. They're closing in on my position and I've got too far to go."

"You can make it. You're almost there."

She stared up at the eye in the sky monitoring everything going on. She smiled, hoping he could see her. "I'm sorry. I know I'm letting you down. I never wanted to hurt you, but we always knew this was a possibility. At least we're getting a chance to say goodbye."

"What? What are you saying? If you can't keep going, just surrender."

She gasped out a cry at the anguish in his voice. "You know I can't let them take me alive, not after what happened. They'll do unspeakable things to me and then they'll kill me. If I'm going to die, it's going to be on my own terms."

"Oh, God, this can't be happening."

She sniffed hard, struggling to maintain control, but her shoulders shook regardless as her chest ached. "You know I love you, right?"

"Of course I do. And I love you. If anything happens to you, I don't know how I'll go on."

She sniffed. "You'll go on. You're going to have a great life. You have friends, family, and coworkers that love you. You're not alone anymore. Promise me you won't go back to the way you were."

"I-I promise."

"I'm going to say goodbye now. Never forget how much I loved you. And if everything goes right, I'll be waiting for you and you can tell me all about the wonderful life you lived."

"I love you so much," he gasped, openly sobbing.

She drew a deep breath and held it for a moment. "Put Sonya on the line."

"Okay."

There was a beep and Tong came on, the woman clearly crying herself. "This is Sonya. What's going on?"

Sherrie spoke her final words, the only ones she could think of that could give the man she loved a future of happiness. "He's all yours now. Take good care of him."

She removed her comms, tossing them on the ground beside her, then raised the pistol to her head and closed her eyes.

God, please forgive me for what I'm about to do.

South of Dauriya, Russia

Jargal stared down at the clearing below, his GPS indicating he was directly over the last reported coordinates for the American agent. The Russians were closing in, he could see them farther down the gentle slope. They would be at the clearing in five minutes. He didn't have time for another pass. He had to take a chance that the American was still there. He banked hard and brought his old girl in for a bumpy landing, cutting his engines in the hopes the enemy wouldn't hear him, the pounding of a nearby chopper potentially drowning out his approach. His rear landing gear touched down then his nose gear, and the skis mounted to them glided along the clearing. He spotted the agent to his left, sitting against a tree, a gun pressed to her head.

"Oh, my God!" He threw open the window as he came to a halt. "Are you all right?" he shouted.

She lowered the gun and stared at him. "Well, you have impeccable timing."

He beckoned her. "Let's go, let's go! We've got maybe two minutes."

She pushed to her feet and hobbled toward him as he fired up the engine and turned the plane around. He impatiently slammed his hand against the door. "Come on, come on, come on!"

She gave him a look. "I'm doing the best I can."

He threw open the door and she climbed in, then he pushed forward hard on the throttle as she yanked the door closed and strapped in. He glanced over at her. "What was going on back there?"

It was clear she had been crying, and he was pretty sure he knew the answer already. She had given up. She was about to take her life before the Russians could, and he didn't blame her. He had heard what they did to men, and that was bad enough, but what they did to women was unspeakable. He reached over and gave her hand a squeeze.

"Never mind, you don't need to answer that."

She pointed ahead. "How about you pay attention to the flying?"

He grinned at her then pulled back on the yoke, sensing he had gained enough speed. They lifted off the ground as gunfire rattled on their port side. He banked hard to the southwest, continuing full throttle, hugging the tops of the trees, then pointed at the GPS with a smile. "Congratulations! You are officially in Mongolian airspace."

The woman sighed, her shoulders slumping, fresh tears rolling down her cheeks. "Thank you, God," she whispered. "Thank you for sending me your angel."

Operations Center 3, CIA Headquarters
Langley, Virginia

Tong sat in stunned silence as Sherrie's last words echoed in her ears. Leroux sobbed at his station, most of the room either crying with him or sitting in stunned silence, uncertain as to what to do. She rose and pointed at Therrien, the next most senior in the room. "You're Control for the moment."

He nodded. "Yes, ma'am."

She wrapped her arms around Leroux, holding the man she had secretly loved for years, a horrifying fantasy coming true in the worst possible way. Sherrie had given her blessing, though that's not why she now held him. Today, she was a friend, and nothing more. Should there be a future for them, it definitely wasn't starting now.

Child sniffed hard behind them, uncharacteristically quiet, his chair still. "Um, has anybody looked at the display?"

She glanced back at him as she continued to comfort her friend, her own tears flowing. "What?"

Child pointed. "I think you're going to want to look at this."

She turned her head and gasped. "Oh, my God. Chris, look!"

He raised his head, rubbing at his eyes as they both stared in disbelief as the small plane whose pilot they had been trying to reach landed in the clearing where Sherrie had spoken her final words.

Tong snapped her fingers at Therrien. "See if you can raise her."

He shook his head. "I'm trying. Her comms are dead."

Leroux gasped at the word then leaped to his feet, crying out with joy at the sight of Sherrie standing and limping toward the plane. He hugged Tong hard, jumping up and down with glee, and she rejoiced with him, though deep inside, part of her mourned for a future of possibilities once again taken away from her.

Yet she would happily make that sacrifice again and again if it meant seeing joy like this on the face of the man she loved.

Mongolia/China/Russia Border
Mongolia

Kane strode toward the decrepit aircraft held together with Gorilla tape, never happier to see such a bucket of bolts in his life, even happier to see a grinning Sherrie staring at him from the copilot's seat. His escape had apparently been less harrowing than hers, having only had to avoid one Chinese patrol before he reached the Mongolian border.

She threw open the door and hopped out, favoring her left leg. He grabbed her in his arms and hugged her hard before giving her a kiss.

"Thank God you're all right."

She grinned, her eyes glistening. "I could say the same about you."

He laughed. "How's that ankle?"

"I'll live, but I did quite a number on it. I'll probably be out of commission for a couple of weeks."

"Weeks is always better than years." Kane shivered. "I hope the heater's good in this plane. I'm freezing my baguettes off."

Jargal gave him a look. "Heater?"

Kane groaned as he climbed in the back. Jargal handed him a glass jar. "What's this?"

"I call it a heater. You might call it moonshine."

Kane grinned and took a swig then gasped, his voice and breath robbed from him for a moment.

"Is it any good?" asked Sherrie.

"Good's not exactly the word I would use. Effective, perhaps." He handed it to her and she took a dangerously long drag on it before a coughing fit ensued.

"Smooth," she gasped.

Jargal grinned. "I told you." He extended his hand and Sherrie slapped it away.

"When you land us someplace warm, then maybe it'll be your turn."

Jargal groaned. "You Americans are no fun."

Sherrie laughed. "Sweetheart, you have no idea how fun I am. And I'm just about to start my second life." She took another swig and handed the jar back to Kane, who regarded her with a smile.

"Just what happened to you out there?"

Tears flowed, and he reached out and took her hand, squeezing it. She sniffed, but smiled, a genuine smile, not something forced for the benefit of others.

"The worst and the best of all possible things."

En Route to Peskov Residence
Moscow, Russia

Peskov sat in the back of his chauffeured government car, his eyes closed, exhausted. His entire body ached. He still hadn't recovered from the shock of Alexei Stepanov trying to kill him with the plunge into the Moskva. He shivered. It had been a bad couple of days, probably the worst of his life. The innocence of his home had been shattered, his children psychologically scarred, and he had secretly betrayed his country, though he was confident for the right reasons. Life would go on, the day's troubles would be put behind them, eventually forgotten, and he and the president, along with their staff, would find another solution to their country's problems.

The president had dismissed him, told him to return to his family and they would discuss next steps tomorrow, and he was grateful for the reprieve. He was already formulating a plan on how to blame Anton Kozak for the failure. He was the one who had left the file with

Victor when he shouldn't have. A fall guy was needed. It couldn't be the president, and it certainly couldn't be him, so Kozak would take the blame. The question was, how harsh would the punishment be?

The car suddenly jerked to a halt and his driver cursed as Peskov recovered, thanking God he had gotten into the habit of wearing his seatbelt even when in the back seat of a limo. "What the hell's going on?"

But his driver never had a chance to answer. Gunfire tore through the windshield and the man shook in his seat. Peskov's jaw dropped as four men approached from a car that had cut them off. Two positioned themselves at the rear windows, assault rifles raised, and they opened fire, splintering the bulletproof glass as he screamed in terror. The armor-piercing bullets made quick work of what the industry called bullet-resistant glass for a reason.

He curled into a ball, covering his head, and sobbed, consumed with self-pity as he realized he was the chosen scapegoat, and likely had been all along. The glass finally gave way and bullets riddled his body as he begged God for forgiveness for every bad thing he had done in his life.

But it was too little, too late.

Leroux/White Residence, Fairfax Towers
Falls Church, Virginia

Kane chuckled as Leroux rushed around the apartment, waiting on Sherrie hand and foot. "Man, you've got to sprain your ankle more often. You're getting the royal treatment."

Sherrie sighed, her still-swollen ankle elevated on the couch. "I can only imagine what he'd do if I got shot."

"You have gotten shot."

She eyed her boyfriend. "You're right. I have gotten shot. He didn't treat me this good then."

"Circumstances were different."

She smiled. "I suppose they were. I feel like I have a second lease on life."

"Me too," agreed Leroux as he rejoined them with a tray of drinks.

Kane's girlfriend, Lee Fang, leaped to her feet to give him a hand doling out the libations. "I guess I'll never know what the hell happened out there, but I'm guessing it has to do with that emergency session of the UN Assembly the other day. What a bombshell that was."

Kane exchanged a grin with the others. "I could tell you, but it would cost you."

"What?"

"A whole lotta loving."

Fang dropped in his lap, wrapping her arms around his neck. "My favorite interrogation technique."

He grinned. "Mine too, but only with you."

Russia and China had both been condemned for what they had attempted, and more sanctions had been brought in. At the moment, there didn't appear to be a conventional weapons deal, but it was an ongoing fear, both parties continuing to deny any nuclear deal had existed, despite all evidence to the contrary.

It didn't matter. The deal was dead, the weapons were back where they were supposed to be, and now would be monitored even closer to make certain nothing like this ever happened again. By blowing up the rail line and the unintended consequence of the detonation of the rockets, it had demonstrated a resolve both the Russians and Chinese had assumed America never had. Hopefully, they would think twice in the future about attempting something so foolish.

Leroux sat beside Sherrie and took a sip of his beer. "So, how did your meeting with Victor go?"

Kane sighed. "A tough one. It's not every day you tell someone the final words and actions of their father, taken thinking they were saving you and not someone wearing a mask that looks like you."

Leroux grunted. "Yeah, that must have been awkward. But he died doing the right thing."

"That's what I told him. He seemed to take it well. He already knew his father had died, of course, but not the circumstances."

"What's going to happen to them now?" asked Sherrie.

"I talked to the Chief and they're putting together the standard package. New identities, bridging financing to get them back on their feet. It looks like the Russians are laying all the blame at the feet of Peskov, so the heat on the Stepanov family might go away eventually. And if we're lucky, that piece of shit running Russia will be dead soon, and then a lot of people's lives can return to normal."

"One can always hope."

Leroux kissed her hand. "One thing I was meaning to ask you."

"What's that, sweetie?"

"After we said our goodbyes, what did you say to Sonya? She's been acting really weird the past couple of days."

Sherrie gasped. "Oh, my God, I forgot!"

"What's that?"

"Oh, you don't want to know, but let's just say I'd better give her a call right now."

THE END

ACKNOWLEDGMENTS

I really enjoyed this one, the subject matter close to my heart. Taking current events and making them the centerpiece of a novel can be risky, in that events sometimes move so swiftly they can change shortly after publication. Should the war end favorably the day this is published, I certainly wouldn't be disappointed.

But books that refer to current events long since resolved when read years later, serve as a snapshot of our times, and I have certainly never regretted past novels that now might seem dated. Some of my favorite James Bond movies are set firmly in the Cold War, where a now-defunct Soviet Union played a critical role in movies like From Russia With Love.

As many know, I work little things from my life into my books, and I had a little fun with this one. There was a girl named Angela, a girl named Thea, a different girl who crossed her 't's uniquely (Petra), and a boy named Ace.

And the COS's mug?

Mother F**ker Who's In Charge.

From my dad's desk when he was commanding officer.

As usual, there are people to thank. Brent Richards for some weapons info, Ian Kennedy for some explosives info, my dad for all the research, and, as always, my wife, daughter, my late mother who will always be an angel on my shoulder as I write, as well as my friends for their continued support, and my fantastic proofreading team!

To those who have not already done so, please visit my website at www.jrobertkennedy.com, then sign up for the Insider's Club to be notified of new book releases. Your email address will never be shared or sold.

Thank you once again for reading.

Made in United States
Orlando, FL
11 May 2023

33048359R00182